THE CHILDREN SEE EVERYTHING

Also by J.C. Hopkins

NOVELS

The Perfect Fourth
All of This
I Was a Teenage Communist
An Extraordinary Turn of Events

POETRY

New York City Love Story
2020 is Hindsight
October to October
Summer of Blue Humidity
From Far Rockaway to Windsor Terrace

THE CHILDREN SEE EVERYTHING

J.C. Hopkins

EPONYMOUS
BOOKS

Published by Eponymous Books
eponymousbooks.com

Copyright © by J.C. Hopkins 2025

ISBN: 979-8-9915091-6-9

Illustrated and designed by Carter Gill
Cover art by Richard Butler

Evil is limitless, but it is not infinite. Only the infinite limits the limitless.

-Simone Weill

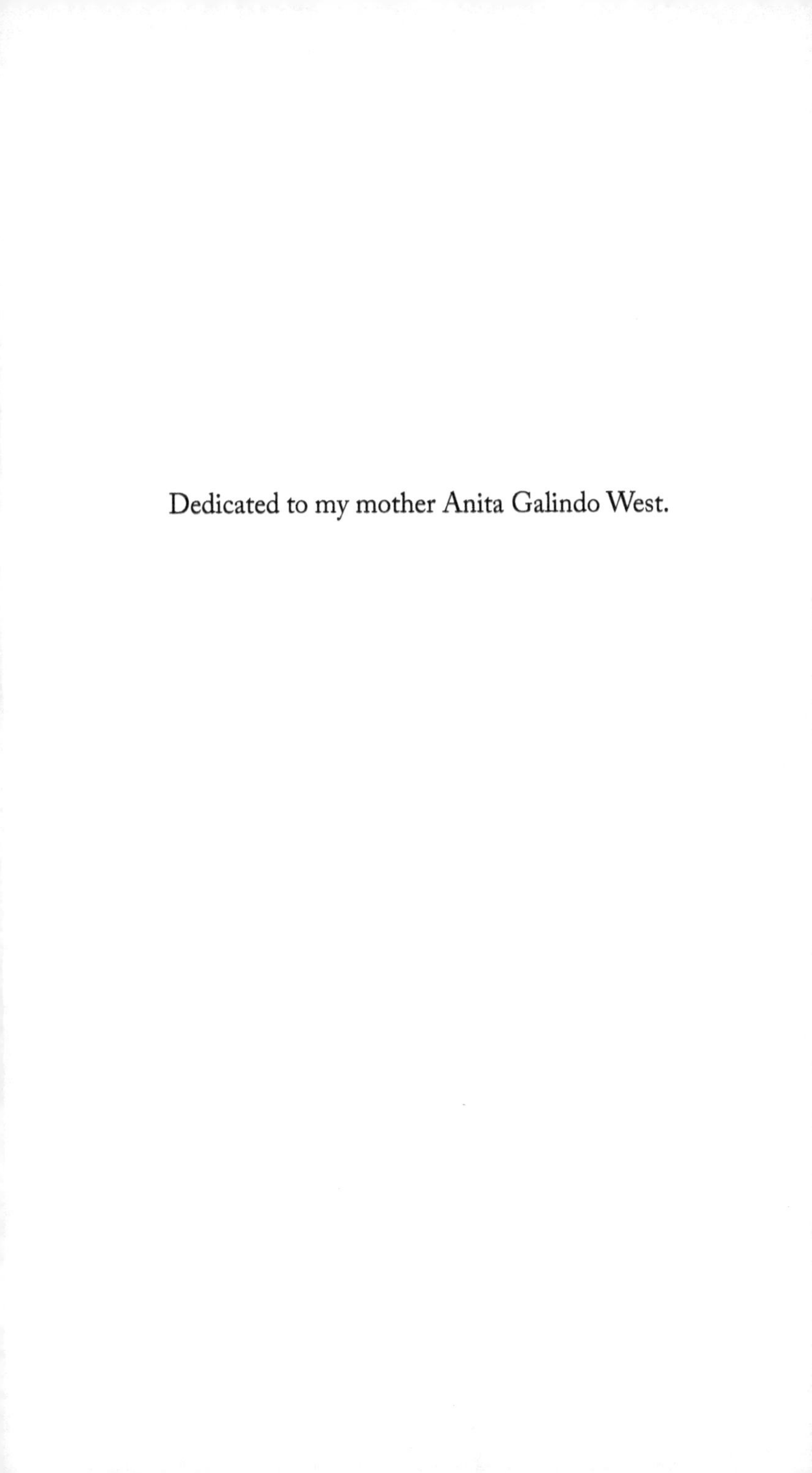

Dedicated to my mother Anita Galindo West.

CHAPTER 1

When Manuel told me he had seen his father kill his mother I thought he was joking. It was a balmy summer evening, still quite light out even though it was almost eight o'clock. An orange haze of smog made a halo around the sun slowly descending behind the San Gabriel mountains. And a cool breeze from the ocean nearby softened the heat of a summer's day, as the incessant sound of katydids added a more unnerving element. I had just had dinner with Manuel's family at their new house. He was walking with me back to mine a few lawns away.

"What do you mean? Are you, are you joking?" I asked him confusedly. The whole thing sounded far-fetched, yet there was no trace of facetiousness in his tone.

"No. I'm not joking. I wouldn't joke about that. I'm telling you because I need to tell someone. You are that someone because you are you." Touching my arm. "But you must not talk about it. Not to anyone." He gave me an intense, if not studied look. "I'm serious. Okay?"

"Okay. But I don't understand. How could that be?"

"I know. Because I saw it with my own eyes. From upstairs, looking through the banister."

"What did you see?"

"There was blood. So much blood."

"What happened?"

"I saw everything. He killed my mother."

"But I saw your mother at dinner."

"She's not my mother; she is my stepmother."

Looking at Manuel I felt like I was looking at myself. I felt an inexplicable affinity towards him. Yet in another way he was completely foreign. I tried to think of something to say. I tried to imagine how I would feel if I was *truly him*. And then my father bellowed my name from through the screen door of our house shattering the quiet between us. "Gerald! Time to come in." Manuel let out a big sigh, stuck out his lower lip and put his hands in the pockets of his shorts. Who was this kid? And again wondered if he was pulling my leg. "Gerald, can I ask you a question?"

"Okay."

"I was wondering. Do you write poetry?"

His question surprised me. "No. Why do you?"

"Yes. But don't tell anyone."

"Okay." I thought, who would I tell?

"I thought maybe you did. Something about your eyes. They listen."

"I write stories. I like to write stories."

"What kind of stories?"

"I don't know. Things from my imagination."

"I wish I had more of an imagination," he said, practically pouting.

"What do you write about? In your poetry?"

"I just put down everything that happens to me. Only I use metaphors. That's what poetry is you know. Do you know what a metaphor is?"

Again, my father bellowed, only louder than before, "Gerald!"

As I turned to go Manuel gently grabbed my arm. "Wait."

"I have to go. I'll be in trouble."

"Okay. But Gerald, I want to ask you something else."

"What?"

"It's hard to say. It's hard to talk about."

"What is it?

He looked down at the ground. "Do you ever think about death?"

"What do you mean?"

"I mean, what happens after you die."

"I guess. Sort of."

"Have you ever lost, you know, a loved one?"

His question, the idea of it, was something I had never really thought about. That's because I hadn't. I hadn't lost a loved one. My grandparents were alive, except my mom's mom, but she died long before I was born, and my parents and my brother were alive and well and, in the house, we were standing in front of. I shook my head. "No."

"That's good. Because once you do you get to thinking about it. You can't stop thinking about it. Where do they go? Is there a heaven and a hell? And all the questions, there is no answer. You just have to guess."

Seeing the anguish on his face. I wanted to be of some help to him. Provide some comfort. "What about the bible?"

"Have you ever read the bible?" he asked me, his mouth a bit agape and eyes wide.

"No. Not really. I've seen the movies on TV."

He smiled and made a couple quiet grunts.

My dad yelled my name from the front of my house and this time he sounded angry.

"I'll see you later," I said. He nodded and walked away. The figure of him, back to me walking to his house, the sound of the katydids, the fading orange, darkening blue sky, this kid, this new kid on the block, different from any kid that I had ever known. But beautiful. Perfect. Perfect in his body, perfect in his sadness. And the saddest thing that could possibly ever happen to someone had happened to him. And in the most terrible way. Yet he seemed somehow removed from it. Many years have passed but still the image of stoicism and resignation in this boy's demeanor, in this boy's melancholy, back to me, returning to a home irrevocably shattered; it has stayed with me.

As I was putting on my pajamas, I remembered that I forgot about my cousin Darrell who died in Vietnam. Was he a loved one? I didn't really know him because he was a few years older than me. But he was always very nice to me. Sweet smile. And he was my cousin by blood, my mother's brother's son. And he was a kid too. I thought of him as a kid and he looked like a kid, but they sent him off to fight in a man's war. And he died. Probably in an awful way. Now there is one less cousin at our gatherings. And when we all got together you could feel his absence like a hole in space. But losing my mom. That was utterly unthinkable.

CHAPTER 2

Lying in bed, trying in vain to fall asleep. Counting sheep, counting down from one hundred, breathing through my nose, filling my belly with air and exhaling through my mouth, all of the tricks my mother taught me to help me get to sleep were not working. Manuel's voice and words kept playing in my head. It was like the story he told me was separate from him, had become its own entity, and he had given it to me, like a book or a photograph or a curse. But it didn't mesh with what I had seen at dinner. Manuel's house was idyllic, so much neater and cleaner than our house, like a Mexican American Leave it to Beaver set. His father resembled Erik Estrada. He had a fulsome head of black hair parted in the middle as if he was a rockstar, and sideburns that went perfectly to the length of his earlobes, immaculately manicured like a grass lawn, and an amiable slightly open-mouthed smile that favored his right side. Only his eyes. His eyes were cold and lifeless.

Manuel's mother, stepmother, was maybe the prettiest woman I had ever seen. But in an artificial, Barbie doll way. She seemed to respond to her husband as if tethered to those cold eyes. But she had an undeniable sweetness to her manner that seemed genuine. Manuel's quiet and reserved little brother, maybe two years younger than him, and as good looking as the rest of the family, sat politely and ate his dinner without saying a word. They embodied the perfect nuclear family.

Our house was messy and chaotic compared to the Pacheco's. Toys sprawled about, my dad's jazz music blasting from his expensive hi-fidelity system, my older brother Kenny never stopped yammering about baseball or politics, the dog was constantly barking or chasing our cat, and because of the dog we were frequently treating the carpet for fleas, the smell of flea spray permeated the house, I was always finding those god damn little black bugs on my skin; Manuel's house seemed immaculate by comparison.

At dinner, Mrs. Pacheco served enchiladas and arroz rojo on bone white China while Mr. Pacheco sat at the head of the table like a lord. So perfect did the food look on the plate I was hesitant to disturb it. The red rice with an array of verdant peas and small orange cubes of carrots dotting the little pile of it, the enchilada covered in a blood red sauce with white and yellow cheese perfectly melted over the top in thin stripes, and bits of forest green cilantro that looked like they were cut from their stems and made to float from on high to where they lay on the dish like little spring leaves.

Before eating dinner Mr. Pacheco said a prayer thanking Jesus Christ for their abundance. Our family never said a prayer before dinner, my father was an atheist. An orthodox atheist was how he described himself to anyone who would listen. Yet, every night, before lights out, my mom, who was not an atheist, or any specific denomination for that matter, at least not until she joined the Unitarian Church, would say a prayer with me and my older brother. "Now I lay me down to sleep, I pray my soul the Lord to keep, and if I die before I wake, I pray the Lord my soul to take; God bless Mommy, Daddy, Papa Joe and Mary Lou, Nana and Grandpa…" And at that point, Kenny and I would list the names of all our cousins, friends, and anyone else we could think of. I wondered how one died before they awoke.

Mr. Pacheco, with head bowed, ardently thanked Jesus Christ for the food and their abundance. How could this man, this seemingly nice and handsome man, this Christian, how and why would he have killed Manuel's mom? And if he did, why wasn't he in jail?

I sat across from Manuel during dinner. He had a be-mused smile on his face in reaction to the conversation, which was mostly his father and I talking about baseball and our local hapless team, the California Angels. His father's voice was like FM radio. It was only when Mrs. Pacheco asked about my school and how I liked going there, that Manuel became fully engaged in the conversation. I spoke sarcastically about my teachers which made everyone laugh, including Manuel. Manuel brought up his old school and how by comparison he liked his teachers, especially his English teacher who had recommended to him the books of C.S. Lewis, the Chronicles of Narnia "I love those books too!" I exclaimed. Having discovered them on my brother's bookshelf the year before.

The whole experience of having dinner with Manuel's family seemed like it belonged in another dimension. Especially after what Manuel had told me.

In the almost pitch-black room, save for my Snoopy night light, I got to thinking about what Manuel had told me, and what he asked me, about death. I thought of the death that I had seen. Mostly dead bugs. Some of them I had personally killed, either by accident or sometimes on purpose. Bugs I had stepped on or rolled over on my skateboard or bike. Caterpillars, their orange guts splurging on the concrete, or the crushing of a snail, feeling and hearing their shell cracking and knowing that life had just gone from it. But you kept riding on. Afterall, you were still alive, and life was for the living. Nevertheless, I had killed and knew what it was like to take life from another being. I hadn't spent much time thinking about it, but it was a fact.

One time I was walking barefoot in the backyard, and I stepped on a black ant. It bit me, hurt terribly. I saw that it came from a small ant hill in front of the garden wall. I went inside the house and put on my sneakers and then I went to the ant hill and stepped down on the mass of them. I stomped and stomped but still they kept sprawling about. No matter how much I crashed down on the ants they kept coming. I kneeled closer to watch them, fascinated by their hyperactivity. And what I saw shocked me. The living ants were carrying away the bodies of the dead ones, risking their own lives in the process. Where were they taking them? What were they going to do with them? Were they going to have an ant funeral? And more importantly, does an ant have a soul?

CHAPTER 3

We should have just rolled in there and killed all of them, I mean all of them." We were at Sid's Steakhouse with the Wersbeys. Jack Wersbey was my father's partner at his insurance firm. Jack's wife Eleanor who looked like she might have once been a model, tall, blonde with a bronze suntan, she chain-smoked through dinner and seemed to be enjoying the wine more than the others. The Wersbey's had two daughters, Emma and June who were approximately the same age as me and my brother. June, the one closest in age to me, sat across from me making funny faces.

Jack said, "Of course, you don't mean that. Even the civilians Robinson?"

My father put a forkful of steak into his mouth, chewed, swallowed, and then took a sip from his glass of Cabernet Sauvignon. "Of course, I do. Every single member of German society was a willing collaborator."

Eleanor said, "What about the children?"

My dad shrugged, "Well, maybe not the children, up to a certain age."

Thirteen-year-old Emma asked, "What age would that be?"

"Conscription age." Dad said, still rhythmically masticating a piece of meat.

"What's conscription?" I asked.

"Don't ask stupid questions," Kenny scolded.

"I thought you were against war?" Eleanor said to my father. "I thought you were a pacifist?"

"Don't be silly. I was against the war in Vietnam. We had

no business being there. Nazis, genocide and the holocaust is a different story."

The Wersbey's didn't seem fazed by my father's pontificating. I imagine they were used to it and even found him entertaining. Like Archie Bunker on the other end of the political spectrum. It was obvious to me he was trying to overcompensate for the fact that Jack was an incredibly handsome man with a beautiful wife. My father had a beautiful wife, but nobody could say he was handsome.

After dinner we drove over to the Wersbey's house. They lived in Huntington Beach near the ocean, in a tract house at the end of a cul-de-sac. As we approached the house, as if by magic their garage door opened and from it the glow of domestic tranquility. "We should get one of those," Mom said. "That darn garage door is so heavy." Jack pulled his Jaguar into the garage. The garage door closed, and Dad parked our Volvo in front of it. The lights in the house turned on and Eleanor opened the front door to greet us.

We walked down the three steps into their living room. Plush wall to wall copper colored carpet filled the floor beneath us like an ocean of shag. Mom, taking in the room, said, "Is that a new sofa?" Jack walked over to the liquor cabinet in front of an all-cork wall. "It sure is, they call it a conversation pit, more like a money pit." He chuckled. Eleanor gave him a dirty look and motioned to the dark orange, velvet, U squared, button tufted sofa which occupied a good portion of the room. My parents sat down next to each other. Eleanor sat down opposite them. "I think night caps are in order." Jack brought over four frosted glasses with gold rings around them, a matching decanter filled with light brown liquid on a wicker tray and placed it on the oblong coffee table made of thick plexi-glass. Eleanor poured drinks while Jack went to the stereo cabinet, opened the lid, and put on some bossa nova music.

This whole scene fascinated me. The women with their long silk maxi dresses made of bright colored floral patterns of yellow, orange, red and brown. Both men wore brown and blue pinstripe suits with wide lapels and thick argyle ties. Each had bushy unkempt sideburns and meticulously coiffed mustaches. The difference was Jack was tall and skinny, and Dad was on the short side at five nine, a bit chubby and wore black horn rim glasses. Their voices were loud and chatty. I felt someone tugging at my shirt sleeve. "Come on," June said. She grabbed my arm, took me down the hall and into her room.

"Get into the closet!"

"What?"

"Get into the closet and when I tell you to come out, come out."

I nervously slid open the door of the closet and got in. June resolutely closed the door. A few seconds later the door opened, and June reached in, grabbed a few dresses hanging near my face, pulled them out and then slid the door closed. I could hear her rustling outside. I tried to keep breathing through my nose as a way of fighting off the anxiety of being shut in a dark closet.

As I sat in the pitch black I thought about my parents and how different they were tonight from how they were at home. My father, even more verbose than usual. My mother, a bit quieter by comparison. But with her long black fake eyelashes, red lipstick and her hair all done up, she looked like a movie star, which was interesting to see. I realized I liked her better as a regular mom than as a movie star. And yet there was something going on I didn't quite understand. The looks which were being exchanged between my father and Eleanor and Jack and Mom had a subtext; the smiles of the men, subtly lascivious, and the expressions of the women bemused.

"Okay. Come out!"

I slid the door open and stepped out. The light of the room had changed, the overhead light was off and just a bedside reading lamp was on pointing in the direction of where June was standing in the middle of the room. She wore a too long dark blue velvet dress, oversized high heels and her hair pulled up with strands hanging down. She had mascara, lipstick and blush applied amateurishly to her face, the expression of which was very serious. She was both puckering her lips and sucking her cheeks in. I wanted to laugh but I knew she would kill me if I did. "Well. What do you think?" I just smiled and nodded. "Now, take notes in your mind of this outfit and then tell me later which one you like best." Confused, I looked her up and down. But my only note was how absurd she looked. "Okay. Back in the closet."

We did this a few times. Each time she mixed some of her big sister's and her mom's clothing. And each time she looked absurd. Finally, I said, "Okay. Now it's my turn." She furrowed her brow. "What do you mean? You're going to put on girl's clothes while I wait in the closet?" I shook my head. "No. Now I am going to dress you. Take off that ridiculous stuff."

She stripped down to her panties. Completely bare from the waist up. Her chest looked like mine except for a scar running down the middle. I searched through her drawers and picked out some white Billy the Kid shorts with silhouettes of eagles embroidered in gold on each of the back pockets. I found a pink t-shirt with the word Pooh written in turquoise across the front; Winnie hugging the P and Piglet sitting on top of the oo's. "I haven't worn this shirt since I was eight," June said incredulously. I made her take down her hair and put it in ponytails. When she had changed, she almost looked normal except for the make-up she still had on her face. "Wash that gunk off your face," I commanded her.

While June went to the bathroom, I went through her record albums. She had a couple Beatles records, the Monkees, Bay City Rollers, David Cassidy, the Lovin Spoonful, and a Partridge Family record which I placed on her turntable. I was thinking that I would have liked to put on some of her clothes if we had kept on playing this game. I often liked to put on my mom's clothes when I knew that she wouldn't come in to find me. Of course, they were way too big, but standing in front of the full-length mirror, with one of her dresses on, I had no trouble imagining what it would be like to be a girl.

My mother often said I had such a pretty face only to amend the compliment by exchanging the word handsome for pretty. My hair was auburn with the red hues inherited from my father, made more prominent from exposure to the summer sun and was a bit longer than other kids as a result of my love for the Beatles. I had a small nose and full lips and a heart shaped chin. I felt both handsome and pretty.

CHAPTER 4

I sat on June's Scooby Doo bed sheets examining the various posters hanging on the pink wallpapered walls. All from Disney movies, each one featuring a perfect white girl at the center of the action of the film. June came back from the bathroom, her face cleaned up, we sat on her bed and listened to the Partridge Family record. "You kind of look like Bobby. Did anyone ever tell you that? You have freckles like he does. Maybe not as many." She put her hand on my hand. "Have you ever kissed a girl?" I stopped myself from telling her about kissing Kathy Baker. I didn't want to make her jealous. So, I didn't say anything. She leaned over and kissed my lips. It made me giggle. She pulled away, "What's so funny?" I shrugged. "I walked in on my parents once," she said. "Yeah?" Not quite understanding what she was saying. "While they were doing it." The record came to an end. June got up, went to the turntable and turned the record over. "Doing what?" I asked. The song *I Think I Love You* came on. "You know, doing it, having sex."

"What did you see?"

In a whisper she told me, "They were naked. He was on top of her, going up and down. At first, I wondered if he was hurting her, and she was moaning, but not like, moaning like she was hurt. Moaning like she liked it. It was weird. I never want to do that. But I would like a boyfriend. Would you be my boyfriend?"

"I don't know."

"What do you mean, 'I don't know.'"

"What do boyfriends do?"

"You know. You know. Like carry my books and walk me home from school."

"But we don't go to the same school."

We looked at each other, very seriously, and then burst out laughing. And then sang in unison, *"I think I love you, but what am I so afraid of…"*

Emma and Kenny came into the room, "What are you guys doing?" Emma turned on the overhead light and put her hands on her waist. "Oh my god, they're listening to the Partridge Family!" Kenny said, taunting us. "So, what!" June snapped back. "What were you guys doing in here and why are my clothes on the floor?" Emma said, picking up her blue velvet dress. "Nothing. Just playing dress up." June replied, a bit embarrassed. "I told you not to mess with my clothes. And mom's high heels. June, you nut!" June got off the bed and started picking up the clothes just to throw them in a big pile. She turned to Emma and said in a low voice, "What are they doing out there?" Emma laughed, "You don't want to know." Kenny sat down on the bed next to me and said, "They have the light down really low and they're smoking something." June and Emma looked at each other and said together, "Marijuana!"

I didn't think it could be possible, and I knew from Kenny's expression neither did he. From everything we had heard from our parents, when the subject of marijuana came up, they were both disapproving. Suddenly the whole night started feeling very uncomfortable for me and I wanted to go home. "Let's play Bloody Mary, Bloody Mary," Emma said.

"You mean Bloody Mary, Bloody Mary, Bloody Mary," June replied.

"Yeah, whatever."

"It's three Bloody Mary's!"

"Yeah. Whatever!"

Before Kenny and I could say anything, the girls grabbed our hands and led us through the house. We had to walk through their parent's bedroom to get to the master bathroom because it was the only bathroom big enough for all four of us, they explained. As we passed their parents' bed, I was thinking about what June had told me about seeing her parents *doing it*. Her father on top of Mrs. Wersbey, naked, him going up and down.

We went into the bathroom. Emma said to Kenny and me. "Okay, tell me the truth. Have you guys ever played Bloody Mary, Bloody Mary, Bloody Mary before?" We both shrugged. "You're not scared to do it are you?" We shook our heads. "What about you June?"

"Heck no. But I want to see her for real."

I asked her, "Have *you* done it before?"

"Just once. But I didn't see anything."

"Well, I've done it a few times," Emma said. "And I've seen her."

"Is she scary?" I asked, biting my fingernails.

"Heck yeah! But she can't get you. She's stuck in the mirror!"

"Let's do it." June said.

Kenny said, "Okay."

"After I light the candle, I'll turn out the lights and then we chant Bloody Mary, Bloody Mary, Bloody Mary and then spin around three times and stop and look into the mirror. We do this three times and on the third time she will appear."

"Who is Mary?" I asked.

"Who is Mary?" Emma repeated.

"Yeah. Who is Bloody Mary?"

"Why, Bloody Mary is Mary Worth. She was a witch executed during the Salem Witch trials."

"Was she a real witch?" June asked.

"Of course not. There's no such thing as witches. Her husband wanted to do away with her and in those days all you had to do was call a woman a witch and they'd hang them. That's why she's so mad and can be easily conjured."

"But she won't hurt us?" June said, sounding scared.

"I told you. She won't."

Emma lit the candle which was on the counter sticking

out the top of a bottle of chianti. Hardened melted wax ran down the neck of the bottle. She turned out the light. In the darkness we would see our flickering reflections in the mirror. Our faces were glowing. As I looked at myself in the mirror, I looked both young and old. It was like I could see myself as an old man. Or even beyond being old. What I might look like on the other side of this life. The room was quiet and because everyone had been so captivated by the tale of Mary Worth, the eeriness of the seance made the air tense.

"Bloody Mary, Bloody Mary, Bloody Mary." We did the cycle three times and on the third time after spinning around the candle blew out. Then we heard screaming coming from the living room. June pushed us aside, opened the door and ran out. We followed her running through the house to the living room. When we got closer, we slowed down and quietly made our way to just outside the living room and stood peeking behind the wall.

We discovered it wasn't screaming we heard, just Mrs. Wersbey's hysterical laughter. There they were, in the conversation pit, the smell of pot in the air, lights dimmed and them recovering from whatever it was which caused them to laugh like that. My father had taken off his glasses and was rubbing his eyes. Jack said, "Oh boy Robinson, you are one funny insurance salesman." And they started chuckling again. All of them except for my mom, who abruptly said it was time to go.

On the ride back Dad was blasting the jazz station on the car radio. "Art Blakey and the Jazz Messengers! A Night in Tunisia a roooonie!" He started playing drums on the steering wheel to accompany Art Blakey's drum solo. Like he was playing conga. And he was really grooving. Usually, his time was not so great, but this time he was feeling it. And right as the solo was reaching a climax my mom switched it off. "Hey!" Dad said. But he sensed she was upset and so didn't say anything. We rode back the rest of the way in silence.

CHAPTER 5

Manuel was a beautiful kid. He had black hair, brown eyes, mocha skin made darker by the summer sun, and his hair cut like Beatle George. He wore nice, clean freshly ironed clothes. He talked gently with a slight Spanish accent. Not like my boisterous Mexican American cousins; they were Chicanos and Chicanas and the way they spoke let you know it. They wore bell bottoms and tank tops, or shirts with the names of rock and roll bands on them. Two of my cousins were just back from Vietnam. One didn't come back. There were a few heated conversations that summer at family gatherings between my father, who was against the war, and cousins Chris and John who had served and recently returned. But it never got so heated that there was ever any bad blood. Somebody would inevitably crack a joke to lighten things. And even though Cousin Darrell had died in Vietnam, nobody felt the need to restrain the conversation. It was what everyone in the country was talking about and had been talking about for years.

We lived in a town called Cypress, formerly Dairy City on account of all the cattle farms which used to be there. The cattle farms left to make room for the tract housing, and that's when they changed the name to Cypress, on account of all the Cypress trees the city planners planted. All the trees and everything else in Southern California came from someplace else. In the case of the Cypress trees, they came from Italy. Phallic, dark green, and cylindrical; more like tall shrubs, going straight up to about fifty feet. And they're hard to climb because they have very thin branches, but the branches are dense, so you can climb them but not without getting full of dust and having small gray pine-cone like seeds go down your shirt. I tried many times. I never got to the top. But I got close a couple times. Eventually I concluded that it wasn't worth it.

Saturday morning, looking in the direction of the television, ostensibly watching cartoons, but I was just trying to digest the information that Manuel had given me. Or expunge it. I wondered whether I had imagined the whole thing. Seemed like our conversation was part of a dream or a nightmare, and if Manuel himself was somebody that I had created. Because I needed a friend. I had wished for a friend and there he was. And he was like me in that he was different from other boys. He wrote poetry. I wrote stories. But what he told me completely threw me. Was it a metaphor? Was he talking in code?

Kenny came in, picked up a pillow and threw it at my head, knocking me out of my stupor. He came over to me, grabbed my arms and shook me, "The kids are gathering at the park for a football game. Come on!"

We passed the Pacheco house on the way to the park a block away from our house. Mr. Pacheco was mowing the front lawn. He had his shirt off and his muscular arms were glistening with sweat. His chest was covered with black curly hair, and more intermittent patches of it on his back. He wore mirrored aviator sunglasses, red swimming trunks and white Adidas sneakers with no socks. The expression on his face was completely blank as he pushed a navy-blue, gas-powered lawn mower with FORD printed in white across the front. It had a canvas bag attached to the side to catch the cut grass. It was even louder when it caught a stick or something hard in the blades, and you could hear the violent sound of the machine chopping it up and spitting it into the bag.

The Park didn't have a proper football field, but the length and width of the grass area was about the same as a regular grid iron. We marked the end zones with traffic cones sniped from a construction site. We played tackle football, not touch, and nobody wore any kind of protective equipment or padding. Somehow none of the kids ever got too badly injured. I was very good at evading tackles. I loved playing wide receiver, going out for a pass, the football arcing in the air like a bird or a bomb, making a great catch and running all the way to the end zone.

The Hanson brothers, who played on the high school football team, joined our game. Rex was the star running back and his brother Troy was the quarterback for the Cypress High Centurions. But for our game they just played on the defense. Troy was tall with blonde hair and looked like Robert Redford. All the kids were kind of star struck around him, but he wasn't arrogant at all. His brother was not as handsome and not as nice. Yet, when the Hanson brothers tackled us, they didn't hit hard. They assumed, when they put their strong arms around one of us smaller kids carrying the ball, we would go down easy. But I would break their tackles all the same and run for the end zone.

The game was tied. My brother was playing quarterback. I was in the backfield. He gave me a hand off and I zigzagged downfield breaking through the arms of the other team. I slipped a little on a loose patch of grass, Rex grabbed me, lifted me over his head and threw me to the ground like a sack of potatoes. I blacked out.

When I came to and looked up at the faces of the kids looking down at me, they appeared as spirits, gauzy, translucent. My head was alternately buzzing and ringing. Troy looked concerned but Rex and the other kids, including my brother had stupid smiles on their faces. "Are you okay?" Troy asked. I was trying to catch my breath and regain my senses. The wind had been knocked out of me. Where was I? Oh yeah, playing football, at the park. I took a few deep breaths and rubbed my eyes. Troy gave me a hand up. I stood unsteadily and took it all in. The world looked altered, more dimensional, not just length, width, height, and depth, but another space beyond, behind the people and things; and a whispering, somewhere in the back of my mind, the words unclear and yet discernible by the sound of them, something about the other world. The quality of the air had changed, the atmosphere had a different hue than before. I saw Mr. Pacheco and Manuel watching from the picnic benches. And then everything snapped back to normal.

CHAPTER 6

August was a tumultuous month. My birthday on the 9th, Manuel's birthday on the 7th and my parents' fourteenth wedding anniversary on August 5th. Cousin Cassandra came over to babysit Kenny and me as they went out to some fancy restaurant. Cassandra was my favorite cousin. She was nice and affectionate, and even though she had patches of bad acne on either cheek I thought that she was very pretty; with long black hair that she wore in braids and short skirts and colorful frilly shirts. She brought a record for me. It was Let It Be by the Beatles. She said it could be an early birthday present. My tenth just a few days away. She knew that I loved the Beatles; my father had four Beatles records, the few rock records in his large collection which was mostly jazz and classical. We went into the living room to listen to it on my father's high-fidelity system. Cassandra said, "I love babysitting you not only because you are my favorite cousin, but because I love listening to records on Uncle Robinson's wonderful stereo."

I loved the record, especially the first song, Two of Us. I thought, Two of Us, Manuel and I, doing all the things that Paul sings about in the song. And the title track, Let It Be; when Paul sang about Mother Mary I thought about my mother, and how whenever I felt sad it was always my mom who lifted my spirits back up. But overall, I found the record different from other Beatles albums; more angry and more melancholy. Cassandra told me that maybe it was because it was the Beatles' last record, probably the last they would ever make. "They look so old," I said looking at the cover, of the four separate pictures, each Beatle in his own box against a black background.

Later that night, in bed, after Cassandra turned out the lights, I felt something hard hit my leg. And then another object hit my chest. I reached down over the side of my bed, picked up a G.I. Joe, and flung it across the room. I heard a groan in the darkness and then a giggle. A wood block hit me in the head. "Ow!" I cried. From there things descended into an all-out war, and because we had our toys scattered messily all over the floor, objects were at the ready to be flung. Kenny said, "Let's have a pillow fight!" He turned on the lights. Even though he was two years older, I was bigger and stronger, which was why I supposed he was constantly challenging me.

We were standing on my bed bouncing up and down going at it and he was getting some good swipes, but he was swinging wildly. He lunged and missed, leaving his head completely exposed. I nailed him so hard on the side of his head that he flew off the bed and landed on a bunch of toys. I walked over and leaned down. I asked if he was all right. His eyes were closed. He looked like he was dead. A series of bubbles, like the kind that came from my Tootsie Toy Bubble Wand, burbled from his nostrils, then dissipated in the air.

His eyes opened. He got up slowly, stiffly and we each went back to bed. I said to myself, "Now I lay me down to sleep, I pray, the Lord my soul to keep…"

The next time I saw Manuel was at his birthday party. The fact that his birthday was two days before mine was another thing we had in common, both of us Leos. My Cousin Cassandra says that I am a Leo with Cancer rising as my ascendant. She says this explains why I am a shy extrovert.

It was just a small gathering of kids mostly from the block and one friend from his old neighborhood. Mrs. Pacheco had gone around to the houses on the block personally inviting the kids. When she came to our house, I was in the living room reading a MAD magazine. Mom answered the doorbell. Mrs. Pacheco stepped into the foyer. Mom asked her if she wanted to come in, but she politely declined saying that she had more houses to get to before getting home to make dinner. As they stood side by side, both wearing summer dresses, they looked like sisters. And even though Mom was older than Manuel's stepmom, she was just as beautiful, maybe even more so as she had a certain confidence that Mrs. Pacheco lacked. Not that confidence makes one more beautiful, but it allows one to move in such a way that draws attention.

In their backyard everything was perfectly decorated. There was bunting along the backyard fence, a birthday banner that went over the swimming pool, the cake, chocolate with vanilla frosting, had *Happy Birthday Manuel!* spelled out on top in red letters. The table had every manner of birthday favors. There were even gift bags for all the kids which contained balloons, water guns, candy, and cracker jacks.

Manuel got a new bike which was on display with a large purple bow tied to the handlebars. It had five speeds, a banana saddle, small wheel in front, big wheel in back, and the same color red as Starsky's Ford Gran Torino. I was a little jealous. I had only recently wrecked my bike jumping trash cans.

Manuel's stepmom lit the ten candles on the cake. We sang happy birthday and then Manuel blew out the candles. All the candles went out except for one which his little brother took care of. And then Mrs. Pacheco cut the cake and went around handing a slice to each kid. As I received my slice, I looked up at her. Golden butterflies danced around her head. She radiated an aura of comic-book beauty. Though there was something disquieted behind her eyes. She smiled, a little nervously and moved on.

After the cake, Manuel opened the presents that the kids had brought, and then Mr. Pacheco presented Manuel with a long narrow box in gold wrapping paper. Manuel slowly, methodically, unwrapped it. He put the box down on the table and pulled from it a BB rifle. All the kids oohed in synch.

Manuel looked astonished as he held it in his hands. Some of the kids asked to hold it and Manuel was only too happy to oblige.

We had a water balloon fight. Then we went into the lima bean shaped swimming pool. All the kids went in except for Manuel and his friend from his old neighborhood. They sat side by side on yellow plastic mesh chaise lounges. From the water I looked at the whole scene, at his dad and his beautiful stepmom, and little brother and all the nice things Manuel had, I almost forgot all of what he told me.

CHAPTER 7

Most of the kids left after the swim except Manuel and his friend from his old neighborhood, still sitting on the chaise lounges. With a towel draped around my shoulders I went over to them, water dripping from my hair. They were intensely engaged in conversation. Speaking Spanish. Hushed tones. Manuel looked up, saw me, and smiled. "Gerald, this is my friend Hector." Hector looked at me and said, "Que pasa?"

"Looks like all the kids left." I said.

"Good!" Hector said. "They were such plebes"

"What's a plebe?" I asked.

"You know, a plebe, a conformist, someone who always behaves as expected."

Hector was a couple years older than Manuel and me, yet he was a little shorter. His skin tawny, jet black hair and a peach fuzz mustache sitting placidly above long narrow lips. His eyes were humongous and when excited they opened wide as his eyebrows arched dramatically. Obviously, he had no shortage of opinions. He looked at me with scrutiny but not unpleasantly. It seemed Manuel had spoken kindly of me to him. "Man tells me that you write stories."

"Yeah. Sort of."

"Sort of! How could you sort of write? You must write as if your life depended on it. No sort of about it. I write poetry, like Man, and one day I will be famous. Why? Because I write the truth. The real truth. The world hates the truth, the ugly beautiful truth, but it also loves it. Man knows."

"Man?" I asked.

"Yeah, Man. That's my name for him because he is already a man. That was put on him."

Manuel led us through the house. We passed his father and stepmother in the kitchen eating birthday cake. They smiled at us. He led us downstairs to the basement which had been converted into a game room. There was a ping pong table, a Pachinko machine, a bench with weights and other gym stuff. Hector said, "Your father is a real *he*-man." There was also a giant TV and a brown leather sofa. We sat down and Hector picked up the remote and started reeling through the channels. Mrs. Pacheco came down and placed two bowls on the coffee table in front of us. One bowl was filled with watermelon slices, the other was for the pits. "Don't get too many pits on the carpet." She said with a kind smile. "Va-voom!" Hector said after she left the room.

We sat eating watermelon slices from one bowl and spitting seeds into the other bowl. Manuel got a few on the carpet. Hector slugged him in the arm but not too hard. "Ow!" Manuel cried. "You heard what the beautiful stepmother said!" Hector flipped through the channels and landed on a war movie. "Man told me he told you." Hector said to me. At first, I wasn't sure what he meant, I had practically blocked it from my mind. But then I realized what he was talking about. I stammered, "He told me something, something about…"

"Yeah, it is hard to believe. I know."

"Well, I don't know Man too good; what I mean is, we have only been friends for a little while. Is it okay if I call you Man too?"

Man nodded.

Hector continued. "Here's the thing. We are just kids. The world doesn't listen to kids."

Man looked at Hector and said, "Hector, I am not saying I should do anything."

"Man, listen to me. Don't even think about it. It's bad

enough you told…what's your name?"

"Gerald."

"Gerald."

Man said, "I don't know what to do."

"What's she like?" Hector asked him.

"Who?"

"Your new mom. I mean your stepmom."

"She's nice. She is really nice to me."

"Does *she* know?" Hector asked.

"I don't think so. No, I don't think so."

Hector slapped his knee. "Damn, she is really foxy."

"Shut up!"

"Don't you think Gerald?"

"Uh, well, she is pretty."

"Pretty! You dweeb. But really. You should have seen Man's real mom. Now she was like Sophia Loren. I mean Jesus Christ. Oh. I'm sorry Man."

"It's okay. Anyone else Hector."

"Wait. You two have probably never masturbated. So, you don't know yet. But I used to think of her. I've been jacking off since I was eight years old. I may be short but in other ways I'm older than I look."

Man was getting visibly agitated. "Just shut up!"

"Okay, okay. I'm sorry. The thing is, not only was she a knockout, but she was also sweet and funny. She always talked to me not like I was a kid; you know how grownups talk to you like you're stupid or something. She never did that. And she gave me books of poetry, Pablo Neruda, Octavio Paz. I'm going to tell you something, and I hope you don't get mad but, I fucking hate your dad. And if I could. I would kill him."

"Me too," Man said quietly. "My mom knew a lot of things. Things that no one else talks about. Things about life and death and how there is so much that we don't know or will never know."

"Wait," I said. "If your father really did what you said he did, why didn't he get in trouble?"

"Because he is a cop," Hector said and then spat some seeds into the bowl.

The conversation couldn't go any further. But there was something in us, something that told us we couldn't let this thing stand. We couldn't let Man's father get away with it. I, of course, didn't know Man's real mom, but the way they talked about her made me feel as if I did.

We sat there eating watermelon and watching a John Wayne movie called The Green Berets on television. Man's father came into the room. He looked down at us, smiled, and looked at the television, "The Duke." On television John Wayne killed a bunch of Viet Cong soldiers. "The Duke just killed a bunch of gooks," he said. "Manuel, let's go and try out your BB gun." Man didn't say anything, just stared at the TV. "What do you say, boys? Want to give it a go?" Hector and I looked to Man, who was not moving. And then more forcefully Mr. Pacheco said, "Let's go!" We got up to leave as the Green Berets theme song played on the television.

Fighting soldiers from the sky
Fearless men who jump and die
Men who mean just what they say
The brave men of the Green Beret

In the backyard, pinned against the fence was a stencil of a man holding a gun and pointing it straight ahead, and over the man's body was a target. Mr. Pacheco handed the BB rifle to Man. "Go ahead son, shoot." Man held the rifle. He looked at us, and then he looked behind him. On the patio was his stepmom and little brother placidly watching the scene. "Come on!" Mr. Pacheco grabbed the gun, pumped it, and made a perfect shot right at the center of the target. "See, it's easy." He handed the rifle back to Man. I looked at Hector who had a strained expression, and then to Man, knowing if he had a real rifle, he would shoot the man who killed his mom. But it was just a BB. A BB rifle wouldn't do anything to a big man like Man's father. Man took the gun, lifted it up, pumped it, and fired. His first shot came nowhere near the target. "Just aim your eye, level with the barrel, son." Man brought the rifle back up and fired again. This time he hit the bird feeder hanging from a tree in front of the fence. He fired again this time, hitting his new bike. "That's it," his father grunted. Man cocked again, but he put the rifle down from his eye and handed it back to his father. "Okay boys, the party is over." Mr. Pacheco walked away, Man watched him as he did, cold hatred in his eyes.

ixlet was obsessed with getting revenge against his perceived enemies, feigning madness only to go mad. Patphelia, was the Ophelia character and Kissonius, was Polonius, sort of; it didn't really follow the Shakespeare play except the parts about madness, paranoia, vengeance, and the contemplation of suicide. The Rosencranz and Guildenstern characters were turned into Woodwardcranz and Bernstienstern.

We had one performance in the backyard on a makeshift stage. Of course, Kenny played Nixlet, after all he had written it. His friend Doug, in one of his mom's wigs, played Patphelia Troy Hanson played Kissonius and Kathy Baker and I played Woodwardcranz and Bernsteinstern.

The play begins with Nixlets' big speech, *To resign or not to resign*. Patphelia rushes in, drunk and ranting, telling Nixlet he can take a flying leap for all she cares. Kissonius comes to Nixlet, tells him he should just bomb a few countries, and he will feel better. Finally, Woodwardcranz and Bernsteinstern tell Nixlet they have written an article for the Washington Boast telling the world of Nixlet's war crimes. Nixlet says, "What a piece of work journalists are." Plunges a dagger into his belly and dies. The play was a hit, especially with my dad.

A couple years before, in second grade, for the 1972 election, our teacher had us make mock ballots, using a copy of a real ballot from 1968 which she illuminated against the blackboard by way of an overhead projector. She crossed out Humphrey and put McGovern. I made mine accordingly and proudly filled in the box for Senator George McGovern. The teacher, Mrs. McAllister was a tall woman with dyed red hair, heavy perfume, and a giant crucifix that hung from her neck between two pendulous breasts. She leaned over my desk, the crucifix knocking me in the head. She smelled like dead flowers. "You made a mistake here honey, you filled the wrong box. Silly boy."

I looked at her, wondering what she was talking about. "No, I didn't," I told her.

"You put McGovern; you are supposed to fill in the box for Richard Nixon." Was she joking? The idea anyone could support Richard Nixon baffled my mind. Little did I know, where we lived, in Orange County, most people supported this president born not too far from Cypress.

"Nixon kills children," I told Mrs. McAllister.

"Excuse me?" she said, less a question and more an accusation.

"Have you ever heard of napalm?" I asked her. Her face started turning the color of her hair.

"What are you talking about?"

Repeating verbatim what I had heard my father say, "Napalm! He drops napalm on children, there are pictures of it, you should see. Napalm is fire, it's like he pours gasoline on children and then lights them on fire." She grabbed my arm, pulled me from my desk and made me sit in the corner of the classroom for the rest of the day. A few days later there was a wooden partition set up in the corner of the classroom. I spent most of the rest of the year behind it.

A few weeks after the ballot incident, my parents sat me down at the dining room table to talk about my report card.

"Gerald, these grades are not good," my father said sternly.

My mom took my hand. "And this note, the teacher made, saying you were misbehaving in the classroom, that doesn't sound like you."

"I don't understand Gerald. D in English. You read more books than I do."

I could feel the tears welling up. "It's because of Nixon," I told them.

My father chuckled. "Well, old Tricky Dick is responsible for many terrible things in the world, but I can't really put the blame on him for your bad report card."

"If your grades don't improve, I don't think we could let you play baseball," Mom said.

I wanted to tell them about the ballot, and the partition that Mrs. McAllister built to put me behind. But I started crying and couldn't get the words out, except for, "Oh please let me play baseball."

I was sitting in front of our house, legs crossed, arms crossed, thinking about how it could be that even though what I was saying was the truth, I got in trouble for it. Maybe if I had told my parents about the ballot confrontation with Mrs. McAllister, maybe they would not be so upset with me, since I was standing up for a good cause, and relent on their threat to not let me play baseball. I knew that no matter how well I did on tests Mrs. McAllister would still give me poor grades.

Man appeared, seemingly out of thin air. "Gerald. Didn't you hear me? I was calling your name." I looked up at him, the way his head was blocking out the sun, eclipsing the sunlight, gave him an angelic glow. "Oh, hi." He sat down next to me. I uncrossed my arms. "What were you thinking about that you didn't hear me calling your name?"

"I was thinking about injustice."

"What kind of injustice?"

"The kind where if you tell the truth you get into trouble."

"Oh. I know what you mean."

"I have heard my parents talk about John Kennedy, Bobby Kennedy and Martin Luther King, and how they told the truth, and they were killed for it."

"And what about Jesus Christ?"

"Is that what happened to him?"

"Yep. The Romans didn't like what he was saying."

"What was he saying? I mean I know a little. But not too much."

"He said, basically, to be kind to your neighbor and help those in need."

"And the Romans didn't like that?"

"And Jesus got mad because they had turned his temple into a market. So, he wrecked it."

"Do you learn all of that in church?"

"Some. Some from books. Some from my mom."

"He sounds pretty cool."

"Yeah. And they nailed him to a cross. Here look." And he pulled out from his shirt a crucifix hanging from a chain. A gold cross, about the size of a quarter, with a little man pinned to it, whose face was anguished, but also peaceful.

"I have seen those. My Papa Joe wears one like it. How does it feel?"

"How does what feel?"

"To wear that around your neck."

"I don't like it."

"Why do you then?"

"My dad makes me. He checks and if I don't have it on, he hits me. Smack!"

Mom called my name from the porch, "GG, time for dinner." We got up. I said goodbye to Man, he walked home. I started to go in. There she was on the porch waiting for me.

Smiling. When I got there, she gave me a hug and said "Dame un besito." And I did.

Poor Man. He had to wear that gruesome thing around his neck and if he didn't his father would strike him. My dad had never hit me. Was that unusual? Was I lucky that my parents didn't hit me or make me wear weird things around my neck? Or were they not acting like parents are supposed to. I thought again, I should probably tell them about the ballot incident. But I knew my dad would go down to the school and make a big stink. Fortunately, I didn't have to. Next Monday upon returning to school there was a substitute teacher. Mrs. McAllister suffered a strangulated hernia and missed the rest of the school year.

CHAPTER 9

Trying to show Manuel how to hit a baseball was like trying to teach my cat how to walk on a leash; not only was he not very good at it, but he also did not want to do it. I had convinced him to play for my team for the fall season. I felt if I worked with him almost every day by the end of September when the season started, he might be decent. At the park, I had a dozen tennis balls I was using for baseballs. "You have to line up your knuckles." I showed him how to grip the bat. He did so. "Then lift it vertically to the side of your ear with your elbow up." He looked good holding the bat. "Okay, now I am going to throw the ball underhand a little, and then overhand after a while." Aside from looking decent, holding a bat, it became pretty evident Manuel had absolutely no talent for baseball.

After we got done, resigned it was a lost cause, we sat on the ground, long grass in our mouths. "You don't have to play if you don't want to, Man."

"Yeah, but now my dad is really pushing it," Man said with a half-smile.

"Just tell him you don't want to."

Man laughed; his dimples prominently displayed. "Oh right. Well, he already knows I hate sports. I guess he is quite disappointed that I am not more macho. I am not good at any sports. I can't even swim."

"That's too bad. You have that really nice pool."

Getting more serious he said, "Tell me about it."

Man, with the baseball bat in his lap, picked it up and

held it like a rifle. "Bang!" He set it down and looking in the distance said, "Have you ever fired a gun?" he asked me.

"No. I haven't. Just a cap gun. Have you?"

"Yeah. It gives a kick."

Nervously I asked, "What gun did you fire?"

"One of my dad's."

"He let you?"

"No. I did it anyway."

"Oh. Did you get into trouble?"

"Yeah. A lot.

"Then why did it seem you didn't like the BB gun you got for your birthday?"

"Just to make him mad."

We sat still for a little while. Man fascinated me. At times he seemed really scared of life and other times he seemed fearless. I couldn't figure him out. And I wanted to. I reached over to Man's lap and grabbed the baseball bat. I put it up to my eye like a rifle and scanned the park. I put it down.

"I wanted a BB gun once. My grandpa said he'd get me a real rifle and show me how to use it. My dad and him had a big argument about it and my dad told him if he got me any kind of gun, he would never talk to him again. So that was that."

"Just as well. If I had a real gun on my birthday, I would have blasted my father's head off with it."

"You would have?"

"No."

"What do you want to happen to him?"

"I don't know. All I know is that my mom is gone, and she is never coming back."

I patted him on the back and said, "I wish there was something that I could do."

"Thanks. You're very nice Gerald. About as nice as anyone. Are you ever mean?"

"Sometimes."

"Like when?"

"Sometimes with my brother. He eggs me on until I wrestle him to the ground. Or I wallop him a lot in pillow fights. Also, the other day I killed a bunch of ants."

"That's all?"

"That's all I can think of right now."

"Okay. Well, I wish I was as nice as you," he said in a funereal tone.

"You seem very nice, to me."

"I have some terrible, terrible thoughts."

"Oh yeah. Like what?"

Man brought his hands together and made his thumbs touch his lips. "Nah, I don't think I should tell you. I don't want you to start thinking that I am not nice. Besides, they're just thoughts."

CHAPTER 10

I was having a recurring dream and in it I am on top of a hill, the heat is coming out of the ground and into my belly, legs and elbows. The sun's heat on my back. I am on the hill looking down to a bluff below me. On the bluff were a group of people wearing khaki-colored robes, huddling together. After a while they start milling about. And then a few long bearded men walked up to the top of the bluff with three men wearing loincloths in tow, bound with ropes, carrying large wooden crosses. They untied the men and then laid them down on the crosses. With the ropes they tied two of the men to the cross. They nailed the other man to his cross. And with each hit of the hammer a most guttural sound emanated from the man.

Lying on my stomach watching, not quite hiding but also trying to make myself not visible to the people below. Perspiration dripped from my forehead. I knew what it was, what it was I was doing, I knew it because I had seen it all before.

After they had nailed the man to the cross, they lifted the three crosses, the two tied ones on either side of the one who had been nailed and slid the crosses into dugout holes. And as the crosses hit bottom with a jolt, the man nailed to the cross let out an anguished moan. The man in the middle, changed from dream to dream; sometimes it was my cousin Darrell who died in Vietnam, sometimes it was John F Kennedy or Martin Luther King, and sometimes it was me. Then it was Man. I felt something hit me on the head, something hard, and then another object hit me on the arm, and then something rather large hit me on the butt. I turned over and opened my eyes. "Happy birthday!" said my brother.

I rubbed my eyes. "What?"

"It's your birthday, stupid. And for it, there is the greatest present."

"Really?"

"Yes, it is the greatest present you could have ever asked for."

"What is it?"

"Come on. Get up!"

I sat up, shook my head to shake off the dream. I stepped into my slippers, and we walked into the living room.

"Happy birthday, sweetie!" Mom gave me a little hug. She was still in her nightgown and robe. My father hollered "Happy birthday son, don't you know it's a great day, Nixon has resigned! Happy birthday!" He did a little hop and gave my brother a high five.

"Wasn't he going to be impeached?" I asked groggily; pleased about the news but also a bit disappointed because it seemed my birthday was to be lost in the mix.

"That's why he resigned. Duh," Kenny said.

Dad said, "Basically, he had no choice. Just as long as he is out of there. The worst president this country has ever had. I remember not liking Eisenhower so much, but in hindsight, Ike was just fine by comparison. You couldn't have asked for a better birthday present."

I did not like Nixon and welcomed this news, still, I did want a few presents aside from Nixon's resignation. And I feared that my birthday would be completely upstaged.

A little later as my brother and I were in our bedroom getting dressed, Putting on my favorite orange Hang Ten shirt, Kenny said, "Do you know what else happened on your birthday?"

"Yeah, I know, Nixon quit."

"Yeah, that, but you know what else?"

"No, what?"

"They dropped the A-bomb on your birthday."

"What?"

"Nagasaki, you idiot!"

"Today?"

"No, moron, at the end of World War Two. First, they dropped an atomic bomb on Hiroshima on August 5th, and then another on August 9th. Who knows when they will drop the next one, but it won't be just one bomb. It will be like one thousand atomic bombs, and hydrogen bombs which are even more deadly, and it will be the end of civilization, those not instantly killed by the bombs will die by radiation poisoning. Hair falling out, coughing up blood. Enjoy your birthday. Who knows how many you got left." Kenny laughed. He finished buttoning his baby blue terry cloth shirt, came over to me, put his arm around me and said in almost a whisper, "Do you know what else happened on your birthday?"

"Um. I don't know."

"Helter Skelter!"

"The Beatles song?"

"No. The Manson Family murder spree began. Charlie Manson thought the song by the Beatles was an anthem for the end of civilization. And maybe it is, who knows? He thought black people would rise up, but they would need a leader, and he would be that leader. So, he told his followers to go to some rich people's house, and slaughter everyone there, and that would kick off the uprising. And they did, they went to Roman Polanski's house, the movie director, he wasn't there, but his pregnant wife, Sharon Tate, and a few other people were, and they stabbed to death the people there and wrote Death to Pigs on the wall in the people's blood. All because of the Beatles' song, `Helter Skelter."

I didn't know what to think. Except Kenny was making something up just to scare me and ruin my birthday.

"All on your birthday. On August 9th," he added.

"You're full of it."

"It's in the book by Vincent Bugliosi."

"Let me see."

"I lent it to Doug."

"You're full of it!" And I ran out of our bedroom and into the kitchen.

Mom was making her signature Mexican breakfast, scrambled eggs with green onions, chorizo, corn tortillas and fresh squeezed orange juice. I put my arms around her and hugged her. She put her one free arm around me. "Hey. Everything ok?" I tucked my face in her apron. She stopped what she was doing and leaned down and saw I had a few tears running down my face. "What's wrong GG?" I shook my head. "Well, don't mind your brother, whatever it is. He's just jealous it's your birthday and not his."

She walked me over to the wicker bar stools at the counter which faced into the kitchen, she lifted me onto one. "I've got to finish making breakfast, but you stay there and talk to me." She went back to scrambling the eggs. "Hey! You're ten years old. I remember on this day, ten years ago, you came into the world. You looked just like an angel. Everyone said so. And you've turned out well if I do say so myself. You're a good kid. So don't let anyone ever use words to scare you or upset you. I will always take care of you." She stopped what she was doing and looked at me. "Okay?" I nodded my head.

We all sat down at the dining room table. Mom picked up her glass of orange juice and said, "Happy birthday GG!" And everyone clinked. Dad had made fresh salsa picante which he poured over his eggs. I put some on my eggs, only to burn my mouth. Everyone laughed. "Not so much meshuga," Dad said. Mom laughed and tousled my hair, switched her plate with mine and gave my father a little smile.

CHAPTER 11

We make myths. We spin macro legends in family. From a very early age we are fed details, anecdotes, delusions, illusions, and we concoct in our minds and imaginations how things came to pass. How you, how I, came to pass. My parents, so different from one another and yet compatible, for a while at least, a while enough to create a family, a home, and fill those people and places with the myth. I'll bite. Or get bit. And I'll take the remedy. Which is what? Rewriting history. The words and images that inform you about you. How you came to be. Who you are. Who you are supposed to be. And yet, no matter, I feel separate, from the history, from the pertinent information regarding my existence. But I am fascinated by it. For a lifetime.

Dad was a heavy-set man with red hair, heavy square framed glasses, and a thick, well-manicured mustache, much like the one that Paul McCartney wore in the Sergeant Pepper days. He often used quaint Yiddish words which my brother and I found humorous. He called me a *gonif* because I often was taking a hammer or a screwdriver from his tool area in the garage, or he said Kenny had a chronic case of *shpilkes* in his mouth. And almost everyone else driving on the highway was a schmuck. When my brother found the book, The Joys of Yiddish, and we discovered the meaning of the word schmuck, we laughed hysterically. Dad was calling someone a penis!

He had no tolerance for things that didn't conform to his aesthetic or sensibilities. Bad food, commercial music, conservative views on politics and culture caused him to seethe. You got the impression that he was one of those people who came fully formed. This was who he was from the second he came out of the womb.

It took him a little longer than most men to become what society calls an adult man. Going to the office Monday through Friday 9 to 5, getting married, home ownership and then, of course, producing children. Up until he was almost thirty years old, he wasn't invested in that particular conception of adulthood. Maybe because he couldn't get the attention from the women he desired. The women that he found attractive rejected him wholesale. And he wanted a beautiful woman. That was important that she be beautiful. He needed that validation. He needed to prove that he could have that, be that kind of man. And if he couldn't have that kind of woman, then he would just do without. Perhaps music could fill that void.

Being an only child, he usually got things his way. He was doted on and poured over and constantly told how special he was. And when he didn't get things just how he wanted, he would throw a conniption fit. Nana chalked it up to him being a ginger. Yet she was a ginger, and I never saw her throw a fit. Or stand up for herself in any kind of way. Even when Grandpa was mean to her and put her down.

They moved around a lot when he was growing up. His father wasn't in the military, he was a structural engineer. They had to go where the jobs were. They lived in Dallas, Seattle,

St. Louis, and Chicago before they moved to California where Uncle Herman found a house for them in Downey. After those freezing Chicago winters, Southern California was Nirvana for Dad.

He attended college as an English major at Long Beach State. He thought, perhaps, that he might be a poet. He loved poetry and read it voraciously. His favorite being T.S. Eliot's, The Wasteland. The poem was Eliot's response to World War One, among other things, but for my father the poem encapsulated his outlook on society. He had been very affected, as a kid, by the daily news accounts of the events of World War Two. And when news of the holocaust became public, it cemented his nascent cynical view of human nature. And it was Eliot's The Hollow Men which served as a sort of anti-anthem:

We are the hollow men
We are the stuffed men
Leaning together
Headpiece filled with straw. Alas!
Our dried voices, when
We whisper together
Are quiet and meaningless
As wind in dry grass
Or rats' feet over broken grass
In our dry cellar

He was determined not to become a hollow man. Yet, he concluded upon reading his first published poem in the Daily 49'er, the college newspaper, that he was a lousy poet. And so gave it up permanently. Then he was drafted into the Korean War.

He spent two years in Okinawa as part of the Stars and Stripes press corp. Not doing much aside from editing the paper and getting into vaguely-alluded-to trouble. The stories he told, when he had a little wine, and his face flushed, and his merriment contagious, not knowing that I was within earshot or even cognizant that I was still at the table or somewhere in the living room lurking about and rapt as he regaled friends. And the stories-were they made up? Seems like I saw some of them on the TV show M.A.S.H..

After serving two years he was honorably discharged. He came back to Southern California and finished his degree in English at Long Beach State. Upon graduating, directionless, he bummed around doing odd jobs only to have just enough money to support his passion for jazz. Uncle Herman called him a no-goodnik.

At that point he was back to living with his parents in Downey. He spent most of his time going to Central Avenue with his friend Tom Halleen with whom he went to Compton High and later served together in Korea. He would often tell me and my brother about seeing some of the greatest names in jazz during that time. "Central Avenue was in South Central Los Angeles. It was called 'the black belt of the city' because starting in the 1940's and after World War Two most of the businesses and homes were populated by Black people, and Central Avenue, where the jazz clubs were, was integral in creating what came to be known as the West Coast Sound of Jazz. People say that the West Coast Sound is a cool, more laid-back version of bebop, but that doesn't tell the whole story. True, there were musicians like Dave Brubeck and Chico Hamilton who were experimenting with combining classical elements with jazz but there were also people like Howard McGee and Gerry Mulligan pushing the envelope of hard bop. I saw and heard them all." He often gave the same speech word for word.

There was another element that the scene came to be known for, and that was heroin. My grandparents started reading in the newspaper about the arrests of jazz musicians for drug possession and they became concerned with how their son was spending his evenings.

One night, after seeing Chet Baker at the Dunbar Club,

Tom Halleen got busted with a couple of joints, one of which he was in the act of lighting in the alley around from the club. Dad wasn't with him but when my grandparents found out what happened to Tom from his mom. They confronted Dad. He insisted that he loved jazz and that was why he went to Central Avenue, not to get high. In fact, he took umbrage they would think so little of him. They accepted this. But they pointed out he was almost thirty and it was time for him to find a direction. Nana asked his brother, Uncle Herman, to help. Herman had made a fortune buying real estate in Southern California in the 1930's. One night he came over for dinner. He told Dad and my grandparents about a very highly regarded business school in Phoenix, Arizona, Thunderbird School of Global Management. If Dad went, Uncle Herman would pay for it.

He said, "Nephew, do you want to do something with your life? Or do you want to be a bum? Opportunity is not luck. Remember that. There is no such thing as luck. There is only taking advantage of the many opportunities which lay before you. I came to California, and I saw an oasis. Most people saw a dessert. It was an opportunity. My parents left Russia because they had the opportunity. And because if they stayed the pogroms would have annihilated them. So, they came to America. They had us kids and then they died. It was not a pogrom that killed them, it was the influenza epidemic. Some might say that was bad luck, but it was not; it was chance. There's a difference. And since I was the eldest, I was the one to take care of your mom and your Aunt Jessie. So, I had to learn about opportunity. I'm giving you an opportunity, don't mess it up!"

On the night before he was to leave for Arizona Tom Halleen paid Dad a visit. My grandparents welcomed him coolly. They very much disapproved of the trouble he had gotten himself into. But they liked Tom, after all he had been my father's friend since high school. And like my dad, Tom was an only child. Tom's father died in a car accident when Tom was in high school and so my grandfather was a father figure to him. His disappointment in Tom was palpable.

After promising my grandparents they would not go to Central Avenue, Dad and Tom drove to McDonald's to get a couple burgers. It was the original McDonald's in Downey. They had been going there since it opened in 1953. They had taken girls on dates there, it was their last meal stateside before shipping out, and now here they were. They sat on a bench beneath the iconic glowing golden arches.

"My lawyer said that I could get two years. Maybe more."

"Jesus Christ Tom."

"Yeah, well, turns out the guy I scored the jays from was a narc."

"Don't they consider that you've never been in trouble before and you served in Korea?"

"Maybe."

They ate quietly for a few minutes.

"They did say if I bought the second joint for someone else. Then they would go light on me."

"If you tell them who it was?"

"Yeah."

"Jesus Christ Tom."

"Don't worry. I'm not going to."

"Well, I didn't tell you to buy me a joint. I just said that if you did, I might try it."

"I guess that's one way of looking at it."

My grandparents assumed that Tom was taking the fall for both boys and felt obliged to do something to help mitigate his circumstances. A drug conviction could ruin his life. They asked Uncle Herman for help in the matter. And again, he came to the rescue. He hired a very good lawyer for Tom. The judge let him off with a warning; if he was busted again the judge would throw the book at him. Tom made the most of his second chance. He got a teaching credential and ended up teaching English and sociology at Cypress High School.

CHAPTER 12

In Phoenix he dutifully attended his classes. He was vice president of the Latin America Club and a vigorous member of Delta Phi Epsilon. Not since the army had he enjoyed such bacchanal pursuits and again mostly in the company of men. He loved dorm life, the drinking, the carousing, the general gleeful fraternization. And despite all his extracurricular activities he did well enough in his studies.

He was on the board of the activities committee of Delta Phi Epsilon and because he knew so much and was so passionate about music, he was put in charge of hiring the bands for the monthly dances. The music was woven into his being, was integral to his identity. Jazz, bebop, was the thing that he discovered, with his friend Tom, and was the thing that determined his view of the world, was his armor, was the thing that colored his consciousness.

He made the rounds of the local jazz clubs. There weren't many in Phoenix. After Central Avenue he was disappointed in what he heard. Still, the groups were competent enough. And it was fun to have a good reason to see the nightlife of Phoenix. What little of it there was.

He was starting to get a bit of a reputation as a concert promoter for the dances. It wasn't only that he was hiring good bands. He was sharing with the musicians some of his records. Music that they had never heard before. Charlie Parker, Dizzy Gillespie, and Thelonious Monk. The music was getting hipper. But not too hip. It was still danceable.

One Friday night, the gymnasium was as packed as it had

ever been, not just alumni and their friends but also quite a few young women from the area came to hear and dance to the music. He took glee in knowing the success of the evening was largely because of him. He received hearty accolades from attendees and a good deal of backslapping from his friends as they basked in the giddy atmosphere. Yet, he was such a nebbish, overweight, freckle speckled ginger in prominent tortoise shell horn rim glasses. He still had trouble getting attention from the opposite sex. At least the kind of attention he craved. But his reputation as a music promoter was becoming a definite thing. And he became more confident talking to women. He got an A for effort in his awkward attempts at flirting with women; because he was so obviously not very good at it, they found him endearing. Endearing and not much more than that.

From the edge of the stage, after performing his master of ceremonies duties, he took in the view of the room with satisfaction. He noticed one young woman sitting at a table near the front of the bandstand avidly watching the musicians. He thought she was easily the prettiest woman there. Prettiest, what did that mean? He often thought about the aesthetics of attraction. How arbitrary it was. Even though he was more often than not rejected by the opposite sex he felt within himself that he was a handsome man. So, he was undaunted. He wondered if there was a key to it, to talking to them. He settled on the nothing to lose approach. He walked over to her, leaned down and spoke.

"I'd ask you to dance but I'm a terrible dancer."

Caught unawares she looked up at him and let out a muted guffaw. She had never seen anyone quite like him. He looked like a cross between Sterling Holloway and Steve Allen.

"That's okay. I can't dance." Her voice was low. Like Lauren Bacall.

"Oh yes. I know it. *I can't dance, don't ask me. I can't dance. Don't ask me. I can't dance mister with you.* Cole Porter, right?"

"No. Jerome Kern."

Right!"

"I really can't dance. I had an accident when I was younger."

"Well, then, you're in luck. I can't dance either. Two left feet. Born that way. The doctors said there's nothing to be done. Do you mind if I sit here?"

"It's a free country."

"So, they say."

He pulled up a chair. He studied her face. His first impression was correct. She was without doubt the most beautiful woman that he had ever seen. Black hair of medium length done like Elizabeth Taylor in A Place in the Sun, beige skin, dark brown eyes, lips lightly painted red and no other discernible makeup. He was transfixed by her. And she was transfixed by the music. "You like the band?" he asked.

"I do. I do. They're good. I've not heard a group from around here play A Night in Tunisia or Epistophy. They may not be that hip, but they play some hip material."

He was taken aback. "You know Epistrophy?"

"I lived in San Francisco for a while and saw Gerry Mulligan with Thelonious Monk at the Blackhawk."

"You, you saw Monk and Mulligan? Wow. What's your name? If I can be so bold to ask."

"You can be. You can be so bold. My name is Rachel. Rachel Gonzales. Pleasure to meet you."

He was still trying to comprehend the confluence of events that led him to be sitting at the table of Rachel Gonzales. So unlike any woman that he had ever met.

"This is where you tell me your name."

"Oh yes. Right. My name is Robinson. Robinson Lerner"

He didn't waste any time telling this gorgeous and musically erudite woman it was he who hired the band and handpicked their repertoire. Not only was she the most beautiful woman he had ever seen, she knew about Thelonious Monk!

After a while her two friends came to the table after dancing. And they too were very attractive. She introduced her friends Elvira and Doris. He stood up and said hello. Doris looked like Grace Kelly. Elvira was very tall and a very good dancer. She had recently moved to Phoenix from Mexico City to study internal medicine at Arizona State. They spent the night chatting. He was on fire, cracking jokes like he was doing a schtick in the Catskills.

As the evening was wrapping up, he offered to give Rachel and her friends a ride home in his 1955 Studebaker. "Thank you. That's very kind. But I have a car."

"What are you doing tomorrow night?"

"I have no plans."

"Would you like to have dinner with me?"

"I don't see why not," Rachel said coyly. And my fate was sealed.

CHAPTER 13

After breakfast Dad told me to go into the garage to get the rope so that he could hang the piñata for my birthday party later in the afternoon. The garage door was already opened, and the Volvo sat in the driveway. I gazed into the garage as the morning sunlight filtered through to a spot, where, illuminated in the darkness, there it was, a brand-new bike exactly like Man's, only mine was pumpkin orange. I ran to it. A stainless-steel gear shifter with a black plastic knob was attached to the top of the bike frame. A voice, my voice, said to me, "It's your first multi-speed bike." I was surprised by the wave of emotion that came over me. I heard sounds of laughter. I turned around, there were my father, mother, and Kenny, beaming at me. My father lit a cigar and walked over to me.

"Like it?" he said.

"Boy, do I ever!" I exclaimed.

"Well, don't break this bike or it will be the last bike you ever get," he told me.

Kenny was smiling. "We'll see how long this bike lasts," he snarked.

And it was true. I was hard on bikes, always trying dangerous stunts. I thought of myself as a wannabe stuntman. I liked to ride over curbs, through puddles, I could jump off the bike while in motion and land on someone's lawn, roll and come up unharmed. The bikes got banged up and eventually wrecked in the process. Yet, my performances were all part of a tangible demonstration of that feeling of invincibility.

Nobody embodied that masculine sense of invulnerability better than Evel Knievel. That's how I wrecked the last bike. Imitating Evel.

Greg Gibson was our Evel. Greg was our daredevil, mad scientist, and demolition expert all wrapped up into one pre-pubescent kid. Greg was fearless. As fearless as John Wayne. He would set up ramps made of wooden planks pilfered from construction sites. Many construction sites all around us. Old ramshackle houses going down, bigger buildings, malls, mini malls, gas stations, going up. Greg would line up empty trash cans, and with his ten-speed Schwinn he'd jump them. His record was eight, but talk was going around that he was going to try for ten.

Earlier that summer the day for the big jump came. As a warmup to Greg, I was going to try and jump four. Greg said to me, "Kid, you don't have to do this, but if you do, I will say that you have a lot of balls, a lot of balls indeed." I backed up my bike some twenty yards, a cherry-red one-speed cruiser, which at this point was a bit too small for me. But it was light. I had already jumped two cans before.

In the films of Evel jumping, more often than not, he crashed on the receiving ramp. The grainy, color saturated film footage would show, at Caesar's Palace or some other venue, Evel revving up the motor, a crowd of hysterical men and women watching, cheering in a state of orgasmic anticipation. He would accelerate in real motion and when he became airborne after leaving the first ramp, the film would go into slow motion. As he made his way over what seemed like a hundred cars, lined up neatly like a row of matchboxes—like a some kind of mythical bird, in his red, white, and blue leather uniform— he'd hit the ramp on the other side. That's when something would go wrong, the front wheel turning in on itself, the bike tumbling, Evel flying over the handlebars, hitting the ground and bouncing, rolling, the bike hitting the ground after him and then hitting him. Then they both skid and slide to a standstill. He lay motionless. Was he dead? No! Just broken. Hundreds of bones broken. He was wiped out. But only for the time being.

I hit the first ramp and was airborne, now I was in slow motion, the kids' faces amazed that I was trying this, a nine-year-old kid, as fearless as Evel. Or as stupid. Hitting the landing ramp, like Evel, my front wheel turning on itself, and like Evel, flying over the handlebars, legs splayed, it was a good thing I was wearing my mother's gardening gloves otherwise my hands would have been ripped up as I landed on the asphalt hands first. As it was, I was a little battered and bruised, but I was fine, to the amazement of the kids—no broken bones. But the cherry-red cruiser's front wheel was bent. Greg told me, "Not bad kid, but the thing is, you gotta keep your arms completely straight and hold on to those handlebars for dear life." *He* cleared the ten cans with no problem.

At that age I felt indestructible, not just from bodily harm but from anything. I felt protected. I felt white privilege, even though I had no concept of the term at the time, and even though I wasn't entirely white. I also didn't register *that* at the time either. But I was white. I presented white. I felt white. Nobody knew my mother was Mexican, nobody who didn't know her, because she had been thoroughly anglicized in a state institution. Or that my cousins identified as Chicanos. Or my grandfather barely spoke English and had come to Arizona from Sonora, Mexico, when he was just ten years old. Like Evel, I felt invulnerable, not just from bodily harm but from the violent forces out in the world. I felt protected by my father's righteousness and my mother, my mother whose affection and love never left me.

And so, I attempted to jump trash cans and to climb Cypress trees. And I believed in my father, that he was right and righteous, even though most of the kids and my teachers did not see things the way our family did, did not think the war in Vietnam was wrong or that Richard Nixon was a crook and a criminal. When my father talked about these things he spoke with such conviction and logic it was difficult to doubt him.

His vehemence made me feel safe, he made me feel righteous.

CHAPTER 14

It was my mother who made me feel loved. Only her. There was an intangible connection between us. Maybe because we had spent a lot of time together in my formative years, while my father was at work and my brother was already in school. We spent many mornings and afternoons in the TV room, watching old movies while she ironed or sorted laundry-so much laundry. As she ironed my father's shirts the steam from the iron gave the air a balmy effect as it dispersed to whichever spot I was occupying.

With her hands she did the work; though not overly feminine, for they were hands that had seen much work, had been scalded under hot water in the kitchen sink nightly. Hands that did the various strenuous chores around the house that involved pushing, pulling, lifting, and carrying. Long fingers, fragrant from soaps and roses, they detected fevers, they caressed limbs aching from growing pains. The hands, a bit bony with veins transporting the life force pulsating beneath the surface, you could touch it, you could feel it, you could see it; the life force in her hands, which were to me the most beautiful and comforting things in the world. Though her hands were a bit roughened there was always a coat of pastel colored paint on the sometimes-chipped nails, like flower petals atop of thorny stems. With her hands she played piano, with me on her lap, or later sitting beside her. Delicately but not tentatively she would play Bach partitas.

She told me she had a boyfriend in San Francisco, before she married my father, a jazz musician, who taught her how to teach herself to read music. It was 1958. She was living and working in San Francisco at a time when that city was particularly vibrant. It was her first job as a hematologist, right out of college. And she landed in a thriving and ebullient city. She felt lucky to be there and working in a large hospital with a state-of-the-art laboratory. It was happening so fast it barely registered that she was an independent, emancipated woman.

After her shift she'd go to the apartment on Russian Hill she shared with two co-workers from Saint Francis Memorial Hospital. Two or three nights a week they'd get dressed up and go to the jazz clubs. The women looked so lavish by today's standards. That was fun. Dressing up. And the men wore suits and ties just to go to the grocery store. Not that they went to a grocery store very often. For men the suit and tie were the uniform going back for decades and decades. But for the women it was imperative to keep up with the latest fashion trends and hairstyles. She and her friends would get home, get gussied up and hit the town.

These young women were crazy about jazz. It made their heads buzz. The music suited the city to a tee. The colors of the clothes and the paint on their faces, on the walls, on the canvases, the neon lights, the traffic lights, and the colors that came out of the horns, the pianos and the elegant singers, it all formed an organic whole.

At the clubs the attention of men was never in short supply. Those men, barely men, felt confident with their expertly oiled hair, with their cigarettes and with possibility. But it was a baritone saxophonist who played at the hungry i that she got serious with. He was a boy from Sweden. His name was Lars. He wore sharkskin suits, had a crew cut, played beautifully and he was crazy about her. On the first night she saw him play, Mom and her friends went with Lars and the other guys from the band to Sam Wo's in Chinatown to get what was essentially their second dinner as it was way past midnight. The food came to them on the third floor by way of a dumb waiter. The wonton soup tasted like dishwater, but they lapped it up all the same. And they talked about movies and music and politics and art. They flirted and ate the bad Chinese food.

Lars and Mom started going out regularly. On the days she wasn't working they would go to museums, movies or to Fisherman's Wharf for seafood like they were tourists. And then she would attend his performances. Her girlfriends liked Lars and the band well enough, but they wanted to go to other places besides the hungry i. So, she'd go alone to see Lars play.

One night he took her to dinner at Ernie's in North Beach. Ernie's was the same restaurant featured in the Alfred Hitchcock movie Vertigo. The one where Jimmy Stewart first sees Kim Novak's character, immediately transfixed and then obsessively so. The waiter uncorked a bottle of red wine and poured it into Lars' glass for approval. He nodded. The waiter poured the wine in my mom's glass and then filled Lars'. They drank and then Lars asked her to marry him. She blushed. Inside felt nothing. And said yes.

They didn't plan a big wedding. Papa Joe couldn't make it, or any of her brothers or sisters. They would go to Arizona at one point and have a second celebration. Lars' parents came from Sweden for the ceremony at City Hall and they all had dinner at one of their favorite restaurants at Fisherman's Wharf. She liked his parents. They were quite jolly, not at all like the Swedish people she had seen recently in an Ingmar Berman film. And his parents seemed to be enamored of her. She was smart and pretty and knew about jazz, the thing their son loved so much.

After dropping off his parents at Hotel Saint Francis, Lars drove her home in his garishly turquoise Delta 88. He parked in front of her place. They kissed for a while, and Lars awkwardly fondled her breast. Lars was always a bit demure unlike his car. She didn't mind, though sometimes she wished that he could be a bit more demonstrative. Lars took out a pack of cigarettes, offered her one, which she declined as she never smoked, took one for himself, put it in his mouth and punched the lighter. In the few seconds that it took for the lighter to pop out a feeling came over her. Not quite foreboding but a presentiment. She felt a shiver, and then something shift inside of her. Lars brought the glowing tip of the lighter to the end of his Chesterfield, inhaled and exhaled a cloud of white smoke. She rolled down her window.

"You know, we will have to move to Stockholm." She wasn't sure if he was talking to her. The way he said it. So, matter of fact. But of course, there was no one else in the car. "Lars, what did you say?" He took another drag, exhaled, and then put out the cigarette in the ashtray. "My parents have a nice apartment for us. It is such a nice city to raise children. You will love it." So bizarre. They had never talked about the idea of leaving San Francisco, let alone moving to Sweden. She looked at him. He was looking straight ahead. This side of him, his profile, she had never studied his profile before. They were always looking at each other. But now he was not looking at her. Almost like she was not there. And this profile, seeing him from this angle, he seemed like a different person. Nothing wrong with the profile. Some, most, would say that it was quite a handsome profile. But cold. His profile seemed cold to her. She realized then, she would never marry Lars.

CHAPTER 15

I took my new bike from the garage, rode down our drive-way and headed to Man's house at the end of the block. It was easily the nicest bike that I had ever had. Maybe the nicest thing that I had ever had. I tested all five speeds; it shifted smoothly and easily. I felt like Icarus. I may not have been entering manhood, but I was becoming a different kind of boy. And I knew that I would fly too close to the sun, eventually the bike would be destroyed. And I would get another bike, though not as nice as this one.

I parked the bike in the Pacheco driveway. The kickstand was attached to the back wheel, not to the frame like most bikes. Another feature I found neat. I walked up to the porch and rang the doorbell. After a minute Mr. Pacheco answered. He was dressed in jeans and a blue T-shirt, but he didn't look casual, he still looked like a doll, like a G.I. Joe. He peered down at me and smiled. "Hello, Gerald, what can I do for you?" He said it not as a question but more as a declaration. "I suppose you are looking for Manuel." I nodded my head.

"Come in. He's in the shower. He will be right down." We stood in the foyer quietly for maybe ten seconds, but it felt like an hour. I could hear the shower running, and then it turned off. Mr. Pacheco raised his voice and shouted up the stairs, "Manuel, your friend is here." Man stood at the top of the stairs with a towel wrapped around his waist and called down, "I will be right there."

Mr. Pacheco led me to the living room and offered me a seat on their dark brown Naugahyde sofa. He sat down next to me. Uncomfortably close. I could hear him breathing. Deep, heavy breaths. He smelled strongly of Old Spice, like he had just come from a shower himself. He leaned down near me, our heads almost touching. "So, you and Manuel have become good friends." I had never had a parent sit and talk with me while I was waiting to play with their kid, let alone someone as intimidating as Mr. Pacheco. I was shaking just a little bit, and I was having difficulty breathing so I decided to hold my breath.

"It's good he met you. He doesn't have many friends. Never has. And then being the new kid on the block, I appreciate that you are his friend. Do you guys have a lot in common?" I shrugged. "A little, I mean, yeah," He looked at me, studied my face. "You're almost as quiet as Manuel. Do you guys talk much between yourselves? Has he told you much about himself?" I shrugged again. "Not really." I let out a big breath. He seemed exasperated. But then he put his arm around me. "Do you want to see something really cool, Gerald?" I looked at him and smiled slightly. My lips felt like they were made of plastic. He got up and walked over to a dark wood desk in the corner of the room. He took out keys from his pocket, unlocked the center drawer, and took out a gun, then he walked back over to me and sat down.

"Have you ever seen a gun before?"

"Not a real one."

"Well, this is a real one, very real. And it comes with special bullets. Do you want to touch it?"

I didn't want to say no, because he might say something about me not being very manly. I reached over to where he held it in his lap and touched it with my forefinger. It felt hard and cold. "Do you want to hold it?" I shook my head. "You see, it has these special bullets, and, well, they kind of explode once they enter a human body. I keep it here for protection. If there were a burglar or a kidnapper, or a serial killer, which it seems like there are more and more these days, I have this. There is a guy called the Freeway Killer. He goes around abducting young boys and he tortures them, tortures their privates, then he mutilates the victim. And there is the Suburban Killer, because you know, he likes the suburbs where it is so quiet and serene, and where people feel safe. People feel safe in the suburbs with their green lawns and hedges. He rapes women and then he kills them. Do you know what rape is? Probably not. You're a nice boy." He picked up the gun, wrapped his hand around it, and put his forefinger through the trigger guard and curled it around the trigger. "Well, with this, this gun, they wouldn't stand a chance."

Man came down and looked at us sitting on the sofa, and then at the gun in Mr. Pacheco's hand. "I was just showing Gerald my gun." Man looked scared. "And I was telling him about the special bullets. You remember about the special bullets?" Man nodded. "Okay then. So, you guys going for a bike ride on your fancy new matching bikes?"

Man, and I rode in tandem through the suburban streets. The sun directly overhead and glinting off the chrome bumpers of the muscle cars parked in driveways. The muscle boys with sleeves rolled up and cigarettes dangling, waxing, or changing spark plugs or just sitting there with the tops down on their convertible Mustangs, listening to Foghat or Boston or Steppenwolf. Man was wearing blue swim trunks, an orange Hawaiian shirt and white Adidas sneakers with black socks going up his calf. We practically matched. We could have been brothers.

The unspoken thing. The gun, we were both thinking about it. The way it looked in Mr. Pacheco's hand. It didn't look too different from a toy handgun I got for my birthday the year before, a black cap gun with a brown handle. And it was on the same streets one day I was riding, waving it around, firing off caps like some suburban cowboy. And as I rode, I saw a woman standing on her driveway shaking out kitchen mats, and I let out a woohoo! She looked up at me, saw the gun, heard the caps going off, screamed, and fled for safety inside her house.

But that gun of Mr. Pacheco's, that was a real gun, and quite possibly the gun that killed Man's mom. I wanted to ask Man if it was, but I didn't have to. I could tell by his expression when he saw it. And the thing that Mr. Pacheco was trying to tell us, was telling us, it was a warning, any idiot could figure that out. But we didn't need a warning, we were already scared. Afterall, we were just kids, and he was a cop. He was a murderer.

CHAPTER 16

"Did you hear about Nixon?" I asked Man as we rode along.

"What about him?"

"He resigned so he wouldn't have to go to jail."

"Oh. No wonder my dad was acting weird."

"He was? Why?"

"He voted for Nixon. Twice."

"What? Why? Doesn't he know Nixon kills children?"

We rode our bikes to the Tastee Freeze. We both got vanilla ice cream cones. Man didn't have any money, so I bought his. He said if his dad knew he rode to Tastee Freeze and knew he had an ice cream cone before lunch, well, then he would be in a lot of trouble. I told him I would be in trouble too, and it's true, only not as much trouble as Man. We ate our cones sitting on the hard plastic orange benches in front of the building which was shaped like a giant vanilla ice cream cone. After simultaneously sticking the bottom of the waffle cone, filled with the last bit of vanilla ice cream, into our mouths, I put the palms of my hands against my eyes and hollered, "Brain freeze!" "Me too," Man grunted out. We stood up, smiled at each other, satiated, and rode our bikes to the park.

We sat on the grass. I could see Kathy Baker riding on her roller skates in the tennis courts. I pointed to her and said, "That's my friend Kathy. She's not really my girlfriend but..."

Man asked, "Have you kissed her?"

"Yeah, I have, a couple times. But it's been a while. Kathy, she lives down the street, right next to your house. One day, we were hanging out in the clubhouse my father built for my brother and me on the side of our house in the backyard and she asked me what you just asked, if I had ever kissed a girl, and at the time the answer was no. And then she asked me if I would like to try, and I said yes. I watched a lot of those old movies with my mom, and they were always, you know, kissing, and so I was curious. And we kissed, and it was nice. And her lips were super smooth, and they tasted, I don't know what they tasted like, maybe a little like candy, maybe that was because we had just been eating strawberry-flavored Starbursts. But something else too. And her eyes were closed and so I thought, do you close your eyes when you kiss? I thought, oh yeah, you're supposed to close your eyes when you kiss. And it was really, really nice. Then I heard a loud banging on the window, which was the window to our bedroom, my brother's and mine, and it was my dad, and he looked so angry. He shouted, 'What the hell are you doing?!' Kathy ran home but I stayed in the clubhouse for a while, afraid to go into the house. When I did, I was expecting my dad to yell at me or something, but he didn't say anything. But that was the last time Kathy, and I ever kissed."

"I've never kissed a girl," he said matter of factly.

We were quiet for a minute or two.

"So, Man," I said, "You don't have to tell me if you don't want to, but I was wondering, how did it happen? You never told me."

"Do you really want to know? Because it is terrible. Really terrible."

"You can tell me."

Man took a deep breath, looked up to the sky and asked me, "Do you love your mom? I mean, really love her."

I didn't have to think about his question for very long because I thought my mom was the most beautiful, perfect person in my world. And not only did I love her, but she was undoubtedly my best friend, even more than Man. We both liked the same kind of movies and TV shows and books and music. And she was always, always there for me. If I was hurt or was sick or was sad, she was there to take care of me, to cheer me up and make me laugh. Also, she would play with me. Often my older brother Kenny would not, or he would be off with his friends and so my mom would play with me. We would play card games or board games or watch old movies on TV. And she was so very beautiful. In a real way. She laughed easily, finding humor in most situations. She would laugh at all my made-up knock-knock jokes no matter how corny. Of course, no one could make her laugh like my father. Which is probably why he lucked out with her.

"Yes," I said, "I love my mom."

"I loved my mom too," he said. "Have you ever been to a Catholic church?"

"No, I don't think so."

"There are all these statues, you know, lots of them are pretty gory. Lots of Jesuses on the cross with blood dripping from the holes in his hands or from the holes in his feet or from the thorns, the crown of thorns that the Romans made him wear, and on his side is a stab wound where the Romans stabbed him with a spear, and it is long and open and the blood is leaking out of it, and if you have ever been to Mexico, to the churches there, it is even worse, way more bloody and scary. And then there are the statues of Mary, and she is so beautiful and sad and loves Jesus. When he is a baby, she holds the baby Jesus—it's called a pieta—and she is so beautiful. That's what my mom looked like."

We sat there for a while not saying anything. Man was crying, just a little; in fact, you couldn't tell he was crying unless you looked at the corners of his eyes.

"They were arguing, which was something that happened more and more. Only it sounded worse than ever. I was sleeping. Our old house was very much like our new house with the bedrooms on the second floor. And my mother was yelling, screaming at my dad, and that's what woke me up. She was screaming at him in this high-pitched voice, and threatening him, threatening to destroy him. I had never heard her sound so angry. I looked at my little brother's bed and he was still asleep, I went to the top of the stairs and looked through the banister at my mother and father down in the entryway, and it happened so fast, so fast. My mom screamed out No! and then my father shot her once in the chest. And it was like her chest exploded. Like when you throw a water balloon, and it hits the ground. Only it was red. And then he stood there, not moving; his face was really, I don't know, like he was, like he didn't feel anything. Eyes dead. Which was the scariest thing. I got up and ran into my bedroom. I don't know if he saw me. I have dreams, and in my dreams, he sees me, but I don't remember him seeing me. I couldn't go back to sleep; I can't really sleep anymore; sometimes I go all night without sleeping." He wiped his eyes.

"After a while, I am not sure how long, seemed like a very short time and also a really long time, I heard voices, a lot of men's voices, and so I got out of bed and crawled on my belly to the top of the stairs and looked down into the living room, and there were all my dad's cop friends, the same guys who would come over when we had barbecues. One guy had a mop, mopping the blood from the tiles on the floor. A few cops were talking calmly with my dad. I saw them put Mom in a bag, zipped it up and took her away. It was a dark green bag. I'll never forget that. The color of the bag, like the trash bags my dad uses when he does yardwork or when he prunes the rose bushes. Yeah, they cleaned everything up. The next morning you couldn't tell that anything had happened."

"They didn't arrest your dad?"

"No. He's a cop, they are all cops. Cops have different laws."

"I don't think so. Do you think he knows that you know?"

"It feels like he does. He has never said anything though, except show me his gun and tell me about his special bullets. I don't need him to tell me about the special bullets.

CHAPTER 17

When I got home, my mother was in the kitchen preparing food for my birthday party. My brother and father were in the TV room watching the news about Nixon. The newscaster's voices, tired, low, monotone. I went into my room and put on a record. The Beatles, Sergeant Pepper.

Listening to the music I let my imagination take me to the places that they sang about. With a little help from my friends—I didn't really have too many real friends, but I did have Man, and my mother, and my cousins. The other boys who lived in the neighborhood were my friends, but they were kind of mean and I didn't feel that I was among them. I didn't get any help from them. I would picture myself in a boat on a river with tangerine trees and marmalade skies, and the girl with kaleidoscope eyes was Kathy, and I used to be mad at my school, the teachers who taught me were definitely not cool, except the librarian Miss Murakami, she would play for me cool records of bands like Queen and David Bowie- things were getting better, I had a friend, a troubled friend, things were not getting better for him- fixing the hole where the rain gets in, seeing the people who disagree and never win and wonder why they don't get in my door- and the girl leaving home, the girl with kaleidoscope eyes, why is she leaving? Is home too much trouble, too violent? Who is the man from the motorcade? and by the time I got around to Mister Kite and the carnival sounds, I heard my mother call my name.

I walked into the kitchen. she was finishing the cake, putting the frosting on it. "Do you want to have the leftover frosting? After all, it's your birthday." She gave me the bowl as she went about rinsing the dishes and bowls and putting them in the dishwasher. She wore a yellow sundress with big white buttons. She made the dress from a pattern taken from McCall's magazine. I sat down on one of the wicker stools at the counter. I watched her work.

"Mom, how old are you?"

She looked at me and smiled. "I am twenty-eight." I thought it was funny every time I asked her how old she was, she said twenty-eight. For as long as I could remember.

"Are all the cousins coming?" I asked.

"Let's see. Uncle Dan and Maria, and I think all the kids. Don't know about John and Chris. And Aunt Ruth and Cousin Cassandra and Camille, your grandma and grandpa, and your friends from the baseball team, some of them."

"And Man."

"Who?"

"Man. Manuel."

"Oh yes, your new friend."

"That's a lot of people."

"I hope I have enough food. But Maria is bringing her delicious tamales, and your father has made a pot of barbacoa. Do you want to help me make the guacamole?" I nodded my head.

She brought down a big green Corning Ware bowl from the cupboard and a brown paper bag of avocados she kept on top of the refrigerator. She sliced the avocados in half and squeezed the green into the bowl. She left a few of the large pits in the bowl. "These pits help keep the guacamole fresh," she said. She gave me a large heavy fork and told me to mash the avocado. I did this as she added more to the bowl. She then added some chopped garlic and onion powder, chopped cilantro, red onion, sliced tomato, some McCormick chili powder, and finally squeezed limes into the mix. Her hands seemed so strong as she got every last drop from those limes.

"This is my father's recipe."

"Are we going to see Papa Joe this summer?"

"Yes, of course. At the end of August, when we always go."

I watched her as she emptied tortilla chips from plastic bags into big wooden bowls. In large glass pitchers she made lemonade from tubes kept in the freezer.

"Mom?"

"Yeah?"

"How old were you when your mom died?"

"Oh, let me see. I was four. Almost five. It was right after my accident, when they put me in the Crippled Children's Home."

"What was her name?"

"Her name was Carmen. Like your Aunt Carmen."

"Do you remember her?"

"A little."

"How did she die?"

"She was doing work for the church, helping the poor. And she caught tuberculosis."

"What's that?"

"It's a disease that mostly attacks one's lungs. But when I had my accident, they found it in my bones."

"Oh. What happened?"

"I've told you."

"I know."

"I fell out of the back of a flatbed truck. Injured my hip. Spent most of my childhood in and out of the crippled children's home. But they had a very good school there. I think I got a better education than my siblings did. I was the first in our family to graduate college, you know."

She poured lemonade into the glass that had Snoopy riding on the Apollo 11 capsule. She came out from behind the counter, held it a few inches away from me and said "Dame un besito." I smiled, she leaned down and I gave her a kiss on the cheek." She handed me the glass of lemonade. "What are your father and your brother doing?"

"They are watching more news about Nixon."

"I kind of feel sorry for him."

My brother walked into the kitchen.

"Who?" Kenny asked incredulously.

"President Nixon."

"Don't be idiotic!" He took out a carton of milk from the refrigerator, took a glass from the cupboard and poured himself a big glass of milk and drank it all in one go, then poured himself another and drank it just the same, and then put the carton back in the fridge, leaving the glass on the counter.

"Kenny," Mom said. Kenny stopped and turned around.

"What?" he said in a surly way.

"Rinse your glass and put it on the rack."

Kenny came back and picked up the glass. Mom grabbed his arm, not harshly but sternly. "Don't ever talk to me that way again. Okay?"

With an almost stunned expression, looking like he was about to cry he said, "Okay, Mom." Kenny turned to me regaining some composure and said, "The Angels are on. Playing the Red Sox."

"Okay."

Kenny left. "Aren't you going to go and watch the game?" Mom asked me.

"Yeah, sure. In a little while." I took a sip from my glass of lemonade.

"So, you really like Manny. It's nice to have a friend so close by. You haven't had a close friend since Bobby moved."

"He doesn't like to be called that."

"Who doesn't like to be called what?"

"Man. He doesn't like to be called Manny."

"Oh."

"His dad is called Manny. Have you met them yet?"

"The Pacheco's?"

"Yeah."

"I met his mom very briefly. When she came to invite you

to Manny's, Man's birthday party. She seems nice."

"She's not his mom."

Looking surprised, Mom said, "She's not?"

"She is his stepmom. His real mom is dead." I wanted to tell her all about it. I even opened my mouth, but the words would not come out.

"Oh, that's sad. Was that why you were asking me about my mom?"

I thought about it, but it wasn't why I was asking about her mom. I was asking her because I wanted to know all about *her*. I wanted to know her story. We all have a story, a story that goes as far as where we are. And I wanted to know my mom's story. But I said, "Yes, that's why I asked."

CHAPTER 18

Sometimes I would tell the kids from the neighborhood that I was not from this planet. That I came from a planet called Glaxis, which existed in another solar system called Migas. My whole family in fact. And that we came to Earth in an exchange for the people who used to live in our house who looked exactly like our family. And I would say this with a straight face and when they told me I was joking, I told them I was not. And it's true. I felt like I was from another planet. But I also watched a lot of Twilight Zone and read my brother's Kurt Vonnegut books. Which inspired my imagination.

Looking at all the people at the party you would think I was a very popular kid, but most of them were my aunts and uncles and cousins. It wasn't that I was unpopular, the guys in the neighborhood liked me enough; I just didn't have any close friends. And the friendships I did have only went so far because I never asked to play with any one kid. I got the feeling most of the kids thought that I was strange. You couldn't blame them, after all I did tell them I was from another planet.

When I told my cousins I was from another planet they asked me which one. Then they would tell me all about the planet they came from. They were very funny and jovial. Both sides of the family. The Mexican and Jewish senses of humor are very similar. Both embrace the absurd. And there was an odd, guarded chemistry between them. The two sides of the family. Both shared immigrant stories. Both sides arrived in America at the same time, around 1910, only through two different borders. So, there was an outsider's sense of things. Though nobody would admit to being an outsider in America.

At the party there was Uncle Dan and Maria and their kids- Chris, John, Danny Junior, and Darlene. They had lost their eldest son Darrell in the Vietnam War. Aunt Ruth and her two daughters, Cassandra and Camille were there. Nana and Grandpa came as did my Aunt Jessie and Uncle Donald and their son David. They came up from San Diego. Uncle Herman came in a big silver Cadillac with his wife Aunt Ozell. I knew I would get a check for fifty dollars from them, a huge sum of money for me and would take months to spend. When my relatives mixed, I noticed that they talked mostly about the weather or food. Until someone cracked the first joke and then the silliness began.

There was a loud bang. Then there was a scream. Then there was laughter. Danny Jr had just popped a balloon behind Aunt Maria. At first, she was livid, her eyes grew wide and her face red. Then as if someone had whispered in her ear that it was all in good fun her face relaxed, and she joined in with the laughter.

Darlene went quietly behind Uncle Herman and stuck a long peacock feather in his hair. He spent the whole party with it there, though I am quite sure he was aware of its presence. The way he held the deadpan expression on his face was hilarious.

We had one of those giant portable swimming pools. Aboveground. Not like the one at Man's house which was in-ground, with a diving board, a shallow end, and a deep end. But ours did the job. And it was deep enough, about 6 feet, though there was not a diving board there was a little platform for diving off.

Everyone was having a good time at the party. The kids were either in the pool or hanging out with my cousin Cassandra in the house listening to records. My cousin Darlene was the only cousin my age; I had a little crush on her, and I knew she felt the same. We shared the fact that we had both been doted over because we were the youngest. And she was very pretty, like one of those Guatemalan worry dolls my Uncle Dan gave me one Christmas. But now that we were a little older, that shared sense of being pampered bonded us.

When we were younger, we would play that we were husband and wife and the pets were our children. At her house were quite a few stray dogs and cats that Uncle Dan had rescued, and birds, fishes, hamsters, lizards, and even a pet garter snake.

One day, a few years before, my mom called me to the phone, she said that somebody needed to talk to me.

"Hello," I said.

"Hello. This is Darlene, your wife."

"Oh, hello honey."

"I have some very bad news."

"What is it?"

"We have lost our baby boy." I could hear her weeping on the other end.

"We have?" Going along but not quite sure what she was talking about.

"Yes. Our boy, Felix, has died. Some kind of disease. We don't know."

"Oh no. That's so sad." And it really was. Felix the hamster had died

The following Sunday we had a funeral in Uncle Dan's backyard. Darlene wore a black dress, and I wore the suit I had worn to my one and only piano recital. All the cousins just wore their regular clothes except Uncle Dan. He wore a black suit, and a white shirt turned backwards. He conducted the service. They had dug a whole and to the side of it was Felix in a Buster Brown shoe box, the lid was off the box so we could pay our last respects. Felix was resting on a white handkerchief, with rosary beads next to him.

Everyone gathered around, the kids sitting on the ground and the grown-ups in lawn chairs. My father didn't come but Mom and Kenny were in attendance. Uncle Dan stood in front of everyone with Darlene and me to the side of him. Uncle Dan spoke. "We are gathered here today to pay our last respects to Felix and to offer condolences to his parents Darlene and GG." There Darlene broke down in tears. I put my hand on her back. But she did not stop crying. Aunt Maria gathered her up. Darlene sat on her lap for the rest of the service. I stood for a minute, feeling self-conscious, and then went to sit on the grass with the other kids. Uncle Dan continued. "Felix was a loving and caring son. He always made people happy. But don't forget, he also had a zany side. He would often climb to the top of his cage and hang upside down like he was a bat. And because of his antics he was given the nickname Wild Thing. He brought joy into all our lives. And now Darrell is going to sing a song in remembrance."

Cousin Darrell stood up from where he was sitting on the grass, picked up a guitar that was lying next to him, walked next to Uncle Dan and started strumming the nylon strings. He sang Yesterday by the Beatles. Star baritone of the church choir, he had a beautiful sonorous voice. Mom and Aunt Maria started to cry. After he finished that song, he said he had one more song and he went into a rocking version of Wild Thing by the Troggs with everyone joining in.

Wild Thing
You make my heart sing
You make everything
Grooooovy
Wild Thing!

CHAPTER 19

They came through the sliding door into the backyard. Man, and his father. Man was wearing dress pants and a white button up shirt. He looked like he was going to church. Mr. Pacheco was wearing white swim trunks, an unbuttoned mustard yellow terry cloth shirt and huaraches. No mirror sunglasses. Not his usual intimidating force of nature. He looked normal. Mom was at the picnic table serving the kids food. Mr. Pacheco introduced himself to her. He had a smile on his face, which made him look even more like a regular dad. I ran over to Man. He had a present for me meticulously wrapped in purple paper. He handed it to me with a little smile. Not much of a smile. And only on one side of his face. I looked at the package, felt the sides and knew that it was a book. I told him thanks and put it on the table with the other presents. Darlene came over. I introduced her to Man. They smiled at each other, and I knew right away that if Darlene had a crush on me, she had a bigger one on Man. She was my cousin anyhow.

When Mom brought out the cake, the top ablaze with candles, everyone gathered around and sang happy birthday. Even my brother. After I blew out the candles my father said, "Happy birthday, son, and what a birthday! Quite an auspicious day." And loudly so that everyone could hear, "This country is rid of the greatest crook in the history of American politics." I saw Mom wince, cousins Chris and John moaned and then laughed. But Man's father said, "You mean the greatest president in the history of America." Before my father could respond, my brother said, "August 9th, everything happens on August 9th—Nagasaki, Nixon resigning…" And then his friend Doug Motley said, "Don't forget Sharon Tate." Kenny said, "Oh yes, the Manson family." He and Doug started singing Helter Skelter. Mom told everyone to simmer down, it was time to open the presents.

I got a glow in the dark frisbee, a football, a new Reggie Jackson model baseball bat, a couple model airplanes; two fighters from World War II, an American Corsair and a German Messerschmitt, which after building and admiring for a day or two we'll load with firecrackers and blow up. From my parents, besides the bike I got another G.I. Joe, the game Battleship, a few packs of baseball cards, and a dartboard. Uncle Dan gave me a goldfish bowl saying he would bring the goldfish on another day. That was okay by me, after all he was the one who brought the piñata. I opened Man's present last. The book All Creatures Great and Small. "It's a book about a veterinarian." I saw Man's father grimace disapprovingly. But I loved it. Between wanting to be a forest ranger and a baseball player I wanted to be a veterinarian. With the doctor's bag that I got from Mom for Christmas and a real stethoscope from her hospital, I would often examine my cat Arnold and our dog Clive. Looking at the book Mom said, "Isn't that nice, what a nice gift." Dad hollered, "And now let's eat the cake and ice cream." Uncle Dan chimed in, "And then the piñata!"

The piñata was the shape of a horse and covered in small strips of colored paper- yellow, pink and red. Uncle Dan told me he had brought it from Tijuana especially for my birthday. Uncle Dan always gave good gifts. Good though odd. For Christmas he would give us old board games his kids had played with, usually missing a few pieces, or maybe some pencils wrapped in tissue paper, or a bag of peanuts, everything wrapped in tissue paper or paper towels he had painted with watercolors. "It's the same for us too," Darlene told me.

Uncle Dan was tall and handsome with a mustache ala William Powell. "A tad eccentric," my mother would say. He

was a handyman by trade. Before that he sold insurance policies, like my dad. But one day he stopped. He said he couldn't
sell life insurance policies anymore. "Paying the rent on death,"
is how he put it. That was after his three older sons went to
Vietnam and then one didn't come back. So, he became a
handyman, but he wasn't too handy. Aunt Maria had to go to
work as a cashier at the supermarket.

Uncle Dan started doing strange art projects, things made
of paper-mâché or wood sculptures that looked like weird
junk. Two by fours hammered together with the nails sticking
out bent and cockeyed. My dad gave him our old Dodge Dart
station wagon when he bought his Volvo. It was in great condition when he gave it to him, but now it had lost all but one
of the hubcaps and had a few sizable dents. His eccentricities
got to be unbearable for Maria. Consecutive nights without
sleep, working on his projects and then sleeping for days. But
the worst part had to do with the death of their son. She never
talked about it. Uncle Dan wanted to talk about Darrell all the
time. She felt, between her sorrow and her husband's men-
tal illness, that she was about to completely lose it, go mad.
So, she kicked him out. Though she loved him a lot, she just
couldn't take it anymore.

Of late we didn't know where Uncle Dan was living. He
said that he was living with a friend in an apartment in Long
Beach, but my mom thought that he was living out of the
Dodge Dart station wagon. But whenever the cousins and
family came over for gatherings, Uncle Dan would pick them
up and they would drive over in the station wagon, though it
embarrassed Maria.

CHAPTER 20

The piñata hung from the rubber tree in our backyard like an effigy. The rubber tree had one long branch that glided over the backyard patio. The rest of the tree leaned against a cinder block wall before climbing vertically, its large green leaves like the wings of some prehistoric bird. Unlike the Cypress trees the rubber tree was a great tree for climbing. I had made a little perch up there and with a pair of cheap plastic binoculars I got for my preceding birthday I would survey the neighborhood. And with the binoculars I would look over the houses at the oil tanks in the distance. I thought to myself that if one were to catch on fire, I would scurry down from the tree, run to the kitchen, and dial 0 on the rotary for the operator and report the fire so the fire department could be alerted right away. I figured I was doing my part in protecting the neighborhood.

Uncle Dan put a blindfold on me and then handed me a two by four about a yard long. "It's your birthday, GG, you get the first hit." He put his hand on the top of my head and spun me around. I headed for where I thought the piñata was, but I could tell by the way everyone was tittering and laughing I was headed in the wrong direction. I changed course, everyone got quiet. I lifted the piece of wood over my head and swung down hard. A direct hit. "Good job," Uncle Dan exclaimed, "Muy bueno, now who wants to go next." He took the blindfold off my head. The piñata was intact. Everyone was smiling, even Man. I walked up to him and handed him the wood. He stopped smiling.

"Go ahead, Manny," his father said, giving him a little push toward the piñata.

"Step forward, son," Uncle Dan said to him. Man stepped forward determinedly, Uncle Dan put the blindfold on him and spun him around. Man lifted the wood, and brought it down hard on the piñata, making a gash. "Okay, muy bueno," Uncle Dan said and moved to take the wood from Man, but Man lifted the wood again and hit the piñata, this time even harder, and then he hit it again and again, he was wild, his mouth twisted, he had made himself bigger it seemed. "Okay, that's enough," Uncle Dan said, laughing. "Just one whack per person!" But Man would not stop; he was hitting it harder and harder until the thing busted open, candy and fireworks falling out of the split horse, both ends falling away from each other. Man was panting. He tore off the blindfold and saw the mess of colored paper and candy on the ground. For a second everyone stood still. Uncle Dan said, "What's everyone waiting for?!" Then all the kids moved in to pick up pieces of candy that had fallen. All except Man. Uncle Dan went up to him, leaned down and said a few words to him. Man grabbed Uncle Dan's arm, looked intently into his eyes, and told him something. Uncle Dan nodded and walked away. I bent over to pick up some pieces of candy. When I looked up, Man was gone.

CHAPTER 21

Mr. Pacheco grabbed Man brusquely by the arm and led him from the party. Darlene told me, "Your friend is very dramatic." For some reason this remark angered me. Though it rang true. At dusk Uncle Dan said that it was time to light the fireworks. I wanted to go to Man's house and plead with Mr. Pacheco to let him come back to the party. I so wanted him to see the fireworks. I knew that he would love Uncle's Dan's display. I told Mom that I was going to get him, but she said that maybe I ought to let Manuel stay home. "He seems like a real nice boy, GG, but there is something about him. I think he is very sensitive and maybe his dad, well, maybe his dad is stricter than yours. Something I sensed by the way he took Manuel home after the piñata. I am sure he is nice, but maybe just a little more strict."

I said forlornly, "He didn't know he was only supposed to hit the piñata once."

There were Big Bangs, Cherry Bombs, and a thing called an Air Torch: you held a piece of wood which was attached to the rocket, you held it high above your head, somebody lit the fuse, the thing made a high pitched wheezing sound, shot up into the air, caught on fire, fizzled and fell to the ground. And there was something called the Burning Schoolhouse, which was just that, a cardboard schoolhouse that flamed up and then smoldered. I loved that one. All combined it was an impressive display. All thanks to Uncle Dan.

After we lit the fireworks, everyone went back inside and had round two of the food. All except the neighborhood kids who had gone home. There were still plenty of tamales, en-chiladas, chorizo, chips and guacamole. My dad whipped up some more margaritas in the blender. Cassandra tried to talk him into giving her one.

"Come on, Uncle Robinson."

"How old are you?

"Sixteen."

"No way!"

"I drink my dad's beer all the time."

"How is Gilbert?"

"Ah, you know. He never gets out of his chair," she said with an atypical tinge of sadness.

"Here you go." Dad handed her a margarita.

"Thanks!" Cassandra brightened. She took a sip. She looked up at Dad with a sideways smile, and then they both laughed. "I want a real margarita."

"Too young."

Cassandra saw me, pointed and reached down into her fluffy cheetah print purse. She came towards me holding a small present wrapped in the Sunday funny pages. "Happy birthday, GG." It was a 45-rpm record of the Beatles song Let It Be. "It's the B side that's extra cool. You Know My Name (Look up the number)." She went over to Dad's super stereo. She took off the Sergio Mendes record that was playing and put on the 45.

I loved the way Dad's stereo looked. When you turned on the Marantz receiver the dials lit up forest green. Cassandra put the record on the turntable, changed the speed and lowered the arm; very delicately because she knew Dad was watching. The song played and it didn't sound at all like the Beatles.

"What the hell is this?" Dad said.

"It's the Beatles," Cassandra and I said simultaneously. All the people in the living room stopped talking and start-ed listening to the song. To the funny voices that the Beatles were singing with. Everyone started laughing, especially when it went into the jazz piano break; someone, presumably the pianist, made funny growly sounds like Oscar Peterson. Even Dad started to laugh. I laughed so hard I fell on the floor. I laughed so hard I forgot about Man and the way he totally destroyed the piñata in a psychotic frenzy. Until I looked up to see Mr. Pacheco talking to my mom in the corner of the room.

He was holding a can of Coors beer, taking intermittent sips. They were fully engaged with each other, as if the rest of the room and all the people were not there. He said something that made her eyes open wide. Then she smiled and nodded her head. She was congenial with him. She smiled at him. That seemed to put him at ease. She had such a beautiful smile; it lit up the room. But it was a performance. I was probably the only person who could tell it was a performance. I knew her better than anyone. Not in a way about knowing all the specific things that had happened in her life, though I knew many of those too, but in a different kind of way. In the way that blood knows blood. I came from her, and she fed me with her body before and after I was born, and she tended to my every need then and now. She shared in my joys and sensed when even the slightest thing was wrong and was able to ameliorate it. I too brought her something, something which helped fill up her life, helped fill up her need to be loved. We all have that. And my love for her, my adoration of her was true and unfixed.

Mr. Pacheco said something and then things tensed up again. She put her hand on his arm. He lightened. She shook her head and pulled back her hand. He smiled, a close-mouthed smile on just one side of his face, like Man. And I had to admit that his dimples were appealing. You could see that. You could see he was charming. He was so handsome; he seemed unreal in many ways.

The sound of the blender grinding ice broke my attention. I looked over to Dad making margaritas, he was watching Mom and Mr. Pacheco.

He finished a batch, turned off the blender, poured a glass, and then dropped an ice cube into a wine glass, poured red wine from a Gallo gallon jug, and walked over to them. Mr. Pacheco walked away just as my father approached.

Mom's smile turned into something else. The kind of look I would see on her face when she was at her desk going over the bills, or when looking at my report card, when my report card was not good, which was more often than not these days. Dad handed her the glass of red wine. She took it and smiled at him, slightly forced. She exhaled. I saw a gold and silver cloud come from her mouth. Dad didn't seem to notice. He said something to her, something that made her laugh.

CHAPTER 22

side from the four Beatles records, the only other non-jazz records in my father's record collection were The Chamber Brothers, Blood, Sweat, and Tears and a Sly and a Family Stone record which was playing loudly on the stereo. I Want to Take You Higher came on, and the room erupted with dancing cousins. Seeing my father and mother side by side, taking it all in; they seemed happy. They exuded a sense of well-being. Even with all the trouble and violence in the world they seemed content. They were a cohesive unit. I had never heard them argue. My father had never raised his voice to my mom. And he had a special way with her, a way of making her smile, a way of making her laugh. When he told a funny quip or joke, first her expression would be that of surprise and then her eyes would light up and she would open her mouth wide and tilt her head back and laugh, staccato, a melody going up and down.

I broke things, like my bike, toys or drinking glasses, other things, more than my brother did, and when I did my father's fury was startling. I sometimes felt like I was being unfairly singled out. That I was being persecuted, even if the accusation was founded. But he never hit me or my brother, not once. I sensed that Mr. Pacheco hit Man.

Since Mr. Pacheco had come back to the party, I figured so had Man. I looked around for him but didn't see him anywhere. I went over to where Mom and Dad were standing.

"Are you having a nice birthday?" Mom asked, putting her hand lightly on the top of my head.

"Yeah. Real nice. Is Man here? I saw Mr. Pacheco."

"You mean the incredible hulk," Dad quipped.

"Mr. Pacheco just came to apologize for how Manuel acted with the piñata. I told him it was fine; he was just having fun." And again, that worried look in her eyes. She put her arm around me, leaned down and kissed me on the forehead. Sly started to sing Que Sera, Sera. Mom sang along. She put her hand on my chin and tilted my head up, so we were making eye contact. She sang to me, "Whatever will be, will be."

I went to the front yard. I could hear the party, the music, talk and laughter going on inside the house. I sat down and took off my shoes. The grass, cool and soft on the ridges of my feet. Ten years old. A decade. A full decade on this planet. I went from a little seed, an embryo, to this boy. I would prefer to stay this way and not become eligible to die for some stupid war like Cousin Darrel. It was fun to play war but in reality, could there not be anything worse? Bullets flying by, comrades slain by your side as you go about trying to kill as many other young men as yourself. Young men like my cousin.

I walked over to Man's house. I wasn't going to knock on the front door or anything, it was late, and the house was dark, but if he happened to be out front, I could check to see if he was okay. I had a bad feeling. Something at the center of my chest. It was making it difficult to breathe. My eyes hurt. What is wrong with me? I thought. Oh yes. The smog. It had been a very smoggy day. You could smell it. It smelled like gasoline. Rotten gasoline. And I had been running around in it. Breathing it in, deep into my lungs.

He wasn't there, of course, and so I went back home. Some of the cousins were loading into Uncle Dan's station wagon. The three younger kids in the back seat, Cassandra, Camille and Darlene, and Uncle Dan, Aunt Ruth, and Maria in the front seat. Uncle Dan yelled out his window, "Happy birthday, GG." And everyone else did the same. Cassandra got out of the car, came over, leaned down and gave me a kiss on the cheek. "You know my name, look up the number." We laughed and she went back to the car.

I went inside. Mom and Dad were cleaning up the house. Picking up the paper cups and plates. I started helping. After we got things pretty cleaned up Mom started doing the dishes. As she stood at the sink, I came over and gave her a hug. She patted my head. "Good news GG," she said. "Maria is taking Uncle Dan back."

CHAPTER 23

That night I was awakened by a tapping on the window above my bed. The same window that looked out unto the clubhouse in the backyard, the same window my father tapped on harshly when he caught me and Kathy kissing. This time the tapping was coming from the outside. It was late, maybe past midnight. I sat up, pushed the curtain aside and looked out the window. It was Man. The expression on his face was strained. "Please, Gerald, can you come out here? It's very important."

I went out the back door where Man was waiting for me. "I have to show you something." He took my hand, held it tightly, and led me. I had never been out this late before. It was quiet, and dark, except for constellations of stars that dotted the sky. Despite Man's alarmed disposition I felt relaxed. The moistened air on my face felt good. It merged with my semi dream state. We walked down the street, and I noticed that Man had a red welt on his cheek. He caught me staring at him and jutted his chin forward.

We walked along the side of his house to the backyard. He put his forefinger to his lips. He led me to a rubber tree. Just like in our backyard. He whispered to me to climb it and told me, "Look past the kitchen to the dining room." I looked at him, head tilted, eyes compressed. But I did what he asked. I climbed the tree. The branch ran perpendicular to the kitchen window. I made sure that I was balanced well and then looked in. "Look into the dining room," he again whispered. I looked past the kitchen, and in the dining room there was Mr. Pacheco, sitting perfectly still, looking in my general direction. Only not looking. Like his eyes were fake, made of porcelain, artificial. Mrs. Pacheco standing right next to him, unmoving. She was completely naked. And yet Mr. Pacheco was not looking at her. He was not looking at anything; in fact, if he was looking at anything, if he focused his eyes through the kitchen and through the kitchen window, he would have seen me cuddling a tree branch.

In front of Mr. Pacheco, on the dining room table was a large silver crucifix, a bible, and the same gun that he had shown me.

After what seemed like an hour but was probably only a couple minutes, I climbed down from the tree. Man walked me back to my house. "Should we call the police?" I spoke timorously. "He is the police," Man responded. I looked at him. I was surprised by how little emotion was in his voice. And he seemed more relaxed than before. Maybe just having me see what he had seen, helped with the burden of the situation. "She's not in danger."

"How can you say that? He had her standing there, naked, and the gun, the gun on the table."

"He is going to kill me. I'm the one who he wants to kill."

"You don't know that. We can't let that happen."

We stopped on my front lawn, and he told me, "When we got back from your house, he took me to my room and he slapped me hard. He told me that I better not forget what he was capable of doing, and if I thought that destroying the piñata was a way of showing him that I was not afraid of him, well then I better rethink that. And I better be afraid of him. Because not only was he capable of hurting me, but he was also capable of hurting anyone or anything that I loved. And that I knew that."

"What if your stepmom called the police on him?"

"She never would. She is as scared of him as I am."

"Do you think that she knows that your father killed your mom?"

"I don't think she thought so when they first got married. She seemed so happy. But now she knows. Don't ask me how, I didn't tell her, but she knows—I can see it in her eyes."

"Is he going to kill her too?"

"No. I don't think so. He killed my mom because she fought back. Esmeralda does not fight back. She's scared of him. My mom was not."

We stood there for a minute. I felt helpless about the situation, Man's predicament. Through the corner of my eye, I thought I saw a shooting star. The stars were out in full force, and the moon was a silver sliver. I purposely let my mind wander; I started thinking about the Ranger spacecraft that had just landed on that little sliver and was now, at this moment, taking photos and sending them back to Earth. The moon seems so far away and yet men, human beings, have gone there. And how maybe they were looking to see if people could live on the moon, because we would need a new planet soon because this one might be blown up any minute in a nuclear war with the Soviet Union. Or be made uninhabitable by the terrible smog and pollution. It's just a matter of a few years. That's what my brother told me. And if and when that happened, all of this stuff about Man and his dad and how he killed his mom wouldn't matter. Wouldn't matter at all.

I pointed up at the moon. "Hard to believe that one of our spacecrafts is up there now, taking pictures."

Man looked up. "Makes you feel small."

"Yeah."

He said again, "I know my dad is going to kill me."

"You don't know that" I said, this time a little exasperated.

And with a very severe look on his face he said, "Yes I do."

"Well then, we have to do something."

"There's nothing we can do. We're just kids."

"Aren't you scared; I mean really scared?"

"I am and I'm not. It's like when you must do something that you don't want to do and you tell yourself that it is just for this time, the time that you're in, and that it isn't forever, it will pass, and it always does. This will pass, this time will pass and then it will be over. But Gerald, listen to me, when that time comes—"

I grabbed his arm, "If."

Man smiled. "If. You must promise not to tell anyone what I have told you. One- nobody will believe you because you're a kid, and two, my father will probably kill you too. Or worse."

We looked at each other intently. It was like looking in a mirror. Not that Man looked like me so much, but we did have something very similar about us, something gentle, even feminine, at least compared to the other kids we knew. Then he smiled, that half smile of his.

I said, "Who knows, maybe there will be a nuclear war before anything happens and then we won't have to worry about it."

He laughed. "I wish."

We said goodbye, and I went around to the backyard and went into the house through the back door. I heard our dog Clive scramble, her claws clacking on the linoleum floor. I went in and she jumped up on me. I patted her and told her to be quiet. I was feeling very unsettled. I went to the kitchen to pour myself a glass of milk, thinking that would help me get back to sleep. I got a glass, the NASA Snoopy glass, from the cupboard, and then opened the refrigerator door and got out a milk carton and took it to the counter. There was a picture on the milk carton. It was a photo of a young boy who looked a lot like Man, like me and Man, a cross between me and Man. I poured myself a glass of milk, drank it down, and poured myself another glass and drank that down too. I took the carton back to the fridge, opened the door, and the light from the refrigerator made a shadow of somebody against the wall of the kitchen next to the fridge. I turned around, let out a gasp and dropped the milk carton on the linoleum floor.

"Just what do you think you are doing?" my father said in a low guttural voice.

"Um, I was thirsty."

"And why do you have your clothes on?"

I looked down at myself. I had my pajama top on, the Yellow Submarine pajamas with Blue Meanies depicted on it, my jeans over the pajama bottoms, and my Vans sneakers.

I looked at him, startled and said, "I don't know."

"You know what I think?"

I shook my head.

"I think that you were sleepwalking. I used to sleepwalk when I was a kid. But it's not true what they say. That you should never wake a sleepwalker. I think it's okay to. I got woken up a few times. In fact, it's the only thing that cures you from sleepwalking. Are you awake now?"

I nodded my head.

"Okay. Let's clean up this spilled milk. Nothing to cry over." He put his hand on my shoulder and smiled.

With paper towels, on our hands and knees we cleaned up the mess.

"Now go back to sleep and we can forget this happened. That is, unless you sleepwalk again. If you do, then we will have to take you to the doctor, and then they will perform an operation that will prevent you from sleepwalking. But we don't want to do that because it is a very painful operation, and you will be laid up for weeks and won't be able to play baseball. Okay?"

I nodded my head but felt he needed to hear my voice, so he knew for certain I understood what he was telling me. I said, "Yes, Dad. I understand."

CHAPTER 24

I wanted to build a better platform in the rubber tree, one to be like the bow of a ship. I had the little stool that I used to keep in the kitchen, which I sat on while playing with toys while my mom did her work preparing and cleaning up meals. I wanted to build something in the tree to place the stool on so that I could spend greater lengths of time up there comfortably, better able to keep an eye on the oil tanks, a few blocks away, in case they caught fire. This was something I was very concerned about. It just so happened I could also see quite clearly the backyards preceding the tanks from the highest perch in the tree. Something that didn't concern me until I realized I could see Man's backyard.

I found the perfect piece of wood, part of a go-cart my brother and I had built which had since crashed and was ruined. I just needed a few nails and a hammer. I could find them in my father's work area in the back corner of the garage. Always a dark and foreboding corner. I was fascinated by it. There were strange paintings and pictures hanging on the wall. One was a blue painting of a gray man standing and looking down at a dead horse. There was a framed black-and-white lithograph of a ship that looked to be lost at sea on a stormy night. There was a bumper sticker that said, "Moby Dick is not a Social Disease." And there was a poster of Marilyn Monroe, completely naked, stretched out on a red blanket.

Above the work bench he kept his tools hanging on hooks plugged into a dotted cork board. I pulled out a stepladder, climbed up and got a hammer. I didn't see any nails on top of the workbench and so I got down from the stepladder and pulled it over to a cabinet. I opened the sliding door of the cabinet and there I found a few cans of turpentine, paint thinner and empty Gerber baby food jars filled with nails and screws. I needed bigger nails, so I rooted around towards the back of the cabinet. I pulled out a red piece of red cloth with ties on either side, and in the middle, a swastika. I knew what a swastika was. I had seen it in the books my brother had about World War II. And I had heard my father talk about the Nazis. I remembered him saying that when we won World War II we should've rolled through Germany and killed every single German because of what the Nazi's had done to the Jews. I didn't understand why he had a swastika. He was a Jew. At least his family was. I put it back and then saw, in the very back of the cabinet an orb, strangely luminescent and pale. I reached for it. It was hard and cold and had two holes in front. I pulled it out and held it in my hands. It was a human skull.

In my frightened, shocked state I knocked over a glass jar of long nails and just as I did my father pulled into the driveway, stopped his car, got out of it and walked into the garage. He stood, peering into the garage, the sunlight behind him made his figure that of a dark shadow. I knew it would be impossible to put the skull back and not have my intentions noticed. I stood on the stepladder, paralyzed. I knew I was in trouble for so many different things: getting into his tools and stuff without asking, breaking the jar of nails, and discovering his hidden, secret items.

He walked toward me. I couldn't move. He took the skull for me and said, "So, you found Homer." He looked at it, smiled and put it back in the cabinet. "Looks like you found some other things. You got dropsy these days. What did I tell you about getting into my things?" I was so frightened that I didn't even realize that I was crying. "Come on, get down from there."

I told him that I was just looking for some nails to build a platform for the rubber tree so that I could keep an eye on the oil tanks, thinking since my intention was one of civic duty, this might lessen his anger. But he wasn't angry. "I suppose you're wondering what I'm doing with a human skull?" I nodded.

I helped him sweep up the broken glass, holding the dustpan and then putting the broken glass and nails on the top of his workbench. "I'll extract the nails later. Come with me." We walked to the patio in the front of the house and sat down at the table beneath a large yellow umbrella.

"It was during the Korean War. In Okinawa, where I was stationed, where there had been a famous bloody battle in World War II. I was walking on the beach one night with my pal Tom Halleen. We had had a few beers I suppose. We came across the skull shrouded in seaweed. We named him Homer. I suppose because we wanted to go home. And we were a little drunk. Homer hung out with us in our barracks, and when it was time to go back to the states, we just didn't think it right to leave him behind, so we flipped a coin, and I won the honor of taking Homer home. But it represented more than just a token or memorabilia from the war; it served as a reminder. I don't know if it is a Japanese or American skull, or some other countryman and it doesn't matter. Some young man died fighting in a war, and all wars are avoidable if men, the men who run the world, had that thing in them that told them right from wrong. It was right for us as a country to go and fight against the Nazis because otherwise even more would have perished. But there should never have been a Hitler. You have relatives, Jews who died in the concentration camps, so unfortunately, we had to fight. But in Korea, which was a terrible and brutal war— well, they didn't have to die; we didn't have to go to Korea, and in the same way, we had no business in Vietnam. Do you understand, son?" I nodded my head. I had heard him talk about these things before at the dinner table or overheard him talking to his friends at dinners and parties. And what he said made sense to me. But I still didn't know what he was doing with the swastika.

"Dad, what about the cloth, with the swastika on it?"

He chuckled. "Well, that was actually used for a skit at a Kiwanis fundraiser. Sometimes you have to be able to laugh at some of the most horrible things."

"Like Hogan's Heroes."

"Exactly."

He helped me build the platform in the rubber tree. After we finished, we went inside and had lemonade. He told me he had a surprise for me. He left and came back a few minutes later with a small black case. "I was going to give them for your birthday but then thought maybe you weren't ready. These are really good ones." I opened the case and pulled it out. It was heavy and solid, certainly not made of plastic. I held them to my eyes. Dad laughed. "Now you can really keep an eye or two on those oil tanks." I never had anything so grown up. On the side of the case were stenciled the words: U.S. ARMY.

CHAPTER 25

It was a Monday afternoon. Kenny was playing a board game called Anzio in our bedroom with his friend Doug. He said it was too complicated for me. That I didn't know enough about World War Two to play. He often implied that I was not smart enough to play the games he and his friends played. I had to beg him to let me join his Strat-o-matic base-ball league. And then I won the championship. Strat-o-matic is a card game where each person playing is a manager and drafts players from the previous Major League season for their team. The player's stats are compiled and put on the cards in terms of percentages regarding hits, home runs, steals, RBIs, slugging, doubles, triples, walks, and so forth; and for pitchers, earned run averages and strikeouts, runs and walks allowed. You roll the dice for each at bat, and supposedly it lines up with the percentages. I won the season because I put together a good team. Kenny had a complete fit and threw the game in the trash.

He was in the bedroom with Doug, and Mom was in her bedroom sewing on the big Singer machine. I could hear the machine's wheel spinning and stopping in short bursts. She made a lot of her own clothes from patterns she got from magazines. Like the yellow dress with the white buttons, I liked so much.

I went into her bedroom. Quietly walked near to her, stood by, and watched her work. She had the TV on, a soap opera, but she didn't seem to be paying attention to it. She seemed both concentrating on what she was doing at the sewing machine, but also lost in thought. After a few minutes I left without her noticing that I came.

I went into the kitchen to make myself a glass of Ovaltine. The kitchen had avocado-green cabinets, a yellow linoleum floor and a red rotary phone hanging on the wall which was ringing. It rang for a while, and since nobody was answering it, I picked up. "Lerner residence," I said. The voice of a woman on the other end, all breathy, said, "Is Robinson there?" It was odd for someone to be asking for my dad. Since it was Monday, of course he was at work. There was a little notepad on the counter by the phone where we were supposed to take down any messages in this kind of situation. I said, "No, he isn't, can I take a message?" There was a pause, and then she said, "Just tell him that his girlfriend called." I didn't say anything and quickly hung up the phone.

CHAPTER 26

Everything was happening all at once. It made my eyes ache. My understanding of the world, the world of adults, was largely informed by the books I read and the movies that I saw but I largely deferred judgment and opinions on most things to them. The adults. My parents. And father cast himself in the role of moral barometer. The woman on the phone obviously had the wrong number. Probably called the wrong Robinson. It would be best not to think about it.

The empty lot used to be a dairy farm, and then the bulldozers and cranes came and cleared it, rubbed it out, as if to efface the past and in the same way the people who had previously inhabited that property. The house, the barns, and the fencing, crushed and then gathered up and hauled away, leaving just mounds of dirt, some broken wood, and holes in the ground. My brother and I used to go and watch it happen. And then we would explore the morass.

That was the year before, before I was allowed to go out bike riding by myself. And now the lot lay empty. Except for the uneven ground, which smelled like manure. And with broken, misbegotten pieces of wood which used to be a barn or a house, my brother and I made a little enclave. But now Kenny no longer came, too busy playing Anzio and Dungeons and Dragons. I would ride and hang out there by myself. Whenever Mom asked me where I went, on those long afternoons of daydreaming, I said to the park. She didn't want me to go to the lot where there were all kinds of dangerous detritus.

One day I took Man over there. It was a hot day, hot and smoggy. Made your eyes burn. And you would rub them with two fingers, back and forth. But you would not be thinking about it being smog that caused the irritation to your eyes. You would not be thinking about the external forces which created your environment. You just took it for granted. You took everything for granted. Your home and how it got there and who paid for it, and the things within it run by electricity and gas, and how and or who enabled those things to provide shelter and comfort and entertainment. And the food that was prepared for you- multiple times a day, magically laid before you without you having to lift a finger. And most of it was made to your tastes and specifications. You just took it all for granted, you didn't think twice or once for that matter. And the same for the smog. You didn't think about how it got there. You just rubbed your eyes and went on with whatever it was that you were doing.

As we rode our bikes through the docile streets, I asked Man how things were going. And then he did something weird, something that I had never seen him do, he laughed. But it wasn't a happy laugh. It was kind of a coughing laugh. An exaggerated laugh. He shouted, "Es lo que hay, es lo que hay." I laughed along with him and said, "Estas loco."

"You'll like where I am taking you," I told him.

"Donde esta?"

"You'll see."

We got there and walked our bikes over the dirt to the one enclave I had set up. I called it an enclave even though I didn't know what that word meant; because it was like a cave and it was almost enclosed. We laid down our bikes and we went in.

"It smells terrible," he said.

"That's because it used to be a dairy farm. Cow poop." He laughed that weird laugh again.

We sat on milk crates that I had found and had made into a sofa. I started whistling the theme song from the movie

Bridge on the River Kwai. Man joined in. He may not have seen the movie because it took him a couple times around to get the melody down. But then he blew hard and strong. He was a pretty good whistler. Better than me. And then he started whistling a harmony. We sounded quite nice. We were making music. And by doing this thing together I felt like I was getting closer to Man, getting to know another side of him, just by whistling. And as we whistled, I saw Kathy Baker heading our way. Kathy, the girl who my dad had caught me kissing. She was wearing a blue dress and sandals, and she was traversing the jagged, rugged terrain determinedly.

She stood before us. Admiring our music. A big smile on her dirt smudged face. We stopped whistling and she applauded. "Nice job!" She looked at me and said, "Who's your friend?" pointing to Man.

"This is my friend Manuel, but I call him Man. He just moved to our block. He's a poet." Kathy looked us up and down, which inexplicably made Man giggle. Kathy stuck her hand above her head. "Nice to meet you Man. You're a poet?" Man nodded. "Well, come on in." I said.

She sat down between us. We sat there looking out over the lot. Perspiration running down our faces. "I think that maybe there are dead bodies buried in this lot." I don't know why I said that except that I had been writing a ghost story and that kind of thing was on my mind. "Really?" Kathy said. I tried to keep a straight face. But I couldn't hold it and burst out laughing. Man started laughing his weird laugh, and Kathy just looked at him like he was a freak. And then she started laughing too. We settled down. "What kind of dead bodies?" Man asked. "Children," I said.

"When I was a real little kid, my mom brought me here, when it was a dairy farm. She had made friends with the wife of the farmer, and she had a kid the same age as me. So, we would come, and they would talk in the kitchen while me and the kid played in the living room. The kid was kind of shy and didn't say much so I listened to what my mom and the wife of the dairy farmer were talking about. One day the boy's mom told my mom that they had sold the farm. That they had been forced to sell the farm, but she was glad because she didn't like it there. My mom asked her why and she said because the farm was haunted. She said that long ago, the first family to build the farm and bring the cows, had taken the land from the Indians who had lived here before. With the help of the army, they killed most of the tribe that was here. They got settled and the farmer and his wife had about ten kids. They lived there many years without an incident. One night, while they were sleeping, they heard some crazy sounds. It was the same tribe of Indians, and they had come to terrorize the farmer. And with the young kids who had since grown up, they rode their horses around the house and beat on drums and chanted and made these strange sounds with their voices- yelps, whoops, and hollers. They would do this every night. There was nothing the farmer could do about it. The Army was not around to help. Off killing other tribes. And it started driving the father a bit crazy. One night he couldn't take it anymore and he went out to confront the Indians but when he stepped out onto the porch they were gone. But the thing was, he could still hear them. Eventually he went so crazy that he killed all of his children and his wife, and he buried them on the farm, thinking that maybe this would satisfy the Indians and perhaps stop them from taunting him. And you know what? It did. After a while, the farmer got married again and had more children. The Indians never came back."

After I finished my story, I realized that I shouldn't have told a story about a wife being killed. Not while Man was there. "Is that a true story?" Kathy asked. I looked at Man who had been transfixed by the story and yet didn't seem to be too upset by it. He had a kind of crazy grin on his face. So, I said, "It sure is."

We sat there quietly for a minute or so. Digesting the story. And I had to admit that it was a pretty good one. And part of it was true. The part about my mom and I coming to visit the farmer's wife and his boy.

"Do you want to kiss?" Kathy said to me. I looked at Man, who looked away. I did kind of want to kiss her. I liked kissing her and kind of thought that I would never kiss her again after my father had broken us up.

Her lips were moist and tasted like cherries. "Do you like my lip gloss?" I looked over at Man. He was staring at us in a kind of fixed stare, but when I looked at him, he looked away. "Am I your girlfriend?" Kathy said to me. Girlfriend. Girlfriend. There was that word again. Is this what my dad did with his girlfriend? And I realized what it meant. I realized that the woman, who was on the phone, what she and my dad did together. I had seen him kiss my mom. Not like Kathy and I were kissing, but then again, my mom was not my dad's girlfriend. She was his wife. Suddenly everything became clear to me. I felt a mixture of confusion, anger, and excitement.

CHAPTER 27

Kathy looked to Man, "You're such a good-looking boy." Man looked to the ground and then to me and smiled sweetly.

"Who would you rather kiss, me or Gerald?'

Man's eyes widened and his lips parted slightly. He flushed. He then regained his composure. He stood up and said, "I better go."

"Where are you going?" Kathy asked.

"I am supposed to be home for lunch and then my stepmom is taking me to get a haircut."

Kathy looked up at Man. "I like your hair. It's so long and black. You look like Paul McCartney." Man smiled or tried to smile. He looked down at us said, "Bye," and stepped out of the enclave. He stood there for a while. As if he was trying to make up his mind. Kathy and I looked at each other. "What's he doing?" she said.

"I don't know," I replied. "Just standing there."

From the enclave, looking out at the back of Man and the rugged landscape beyond; it looked like a painting. The back of Man's clean white shirt, his gray shorts that went to the middle of his thigh, the sun-stained dark skin of his legs that blended into black socks that sat three quarters up his calf, that led to his black and white Adidas sneakers. Even his backside was beautiful, poised and immaculate. His head we couldn't see, cut off by the top of the fort.

Then something hit him hard in the chest. The sound of it, like a dull thud. He lurched back, off balanced, staggered, regained his equilibrium, turned, and rushed back into the enclave. He sat down next to us, and he turned to me; his eyes wide, eyebrows arched and the corners of his mouth downturned. Another hard object fell at my feet. I picked it up. It was a dirt clod the size of a golf ball. A few more started coming in and hitting the old boards my brother and I had used for the roof. Kathy picked up a few clods lying at her feet, stepped out of the fort, and threw them to where the clods were coming from, behind dirt mounds about fifty feet away. She fired one off, it had speed and accuracy, and it hit a kid in the face. He screamed. The dirt clods stopped coming in. Man, and I stepped further out of the fort, our hands holding dirt clods, ready to launch. Kathy pointed out to where there were two kids. One was looking at the face of the other. It was Doug and my brother, and it was my brother who got hit in the face. He started to cry and ran off.

Man looked down at his shirt. There was a big dark mark where the first dirt clod had hit. "I am going to be in so much trouble. My stepmom just bought this shirt for me." It was a pristine white pocket t-shirt. Very cool, very nice shirt. I envied him this shirt. I felt bad for Man. "My dad is going to kill me."

We walked our bikes back, Kathy walking alongside us. "Why would your dad kill you? You're a boy. Boys get dirty and wreck their clothes. I have an older brother, and he wrecks his clothes all the time." I looked at Man. He looked like he was about to cry. "Is your dad real strict or something?" Man didn't say anything. It was like he couldn't hear. He just looked straight ahead.

"His dad is a cop," I told Kathy.

"What's he going to do? Arrest him?" And she laughed. Not a mean laugh, not a laugh that was making fun of Man, but just as a way of trying to lighten the situation. I chuckled a little too. But I was scared. I was scared for Man.

We got to his house. He walked morosely up the driveway. He stopped a few feet from his front door, turned around and gave us a little wave. I think he knew that no matter what, we were his friends. And from his expression, his sad, thoughtful, expression, I could tell that knowledge gave him some peace of mind.

Kathy and I walked on. Her house was between Man's and mine. "You really nailed my brother." She looked down at the ground. "It was a pretty good throw." She smiled coyly. "I hope he's all right. He sure was wailing. But it was just a dirt clod. No rock in the middle. I wouldn't throw a rock. Still, I'm sorry." She said she was sorry, but I could tell that she really wasn't sorry. I tried to think about how I felt. Did I feel bad for him? My brother. And I tried to know what I was feeling, but I concluded I wasn't feeling anything about it one way or another. I admired Kathy. It was a really great throw.

I walked into my house, to the left was a white partition made of circles within squares, and then the living room. Wall to wall beige shag carpet, a light blue Ethan Allen wraparound sofa with a coffee table in front of it that faced the front windows and a gas fireplace. Above the fireplace was a painting of a lady with a long neck, just a black line drawing on a red background. "Modigliani's girlfriend," Is what my dad said when I asked him who it was. Kenny on the sofa. My mom was holding a washcloth on his face. Mom looked at me when I came in. She looked very upset. I couldn't tell if Kenny had seen me, knew it was me with Kathy at the enclave, and if he knew; had he told Mom? I decided to play it cool.

"What happened?" I said.

"Your brother got hit in the face with a baseball."

CHAPTER 28

It was nighttime by the time we got to Interstate 10 and the long stretch of highway which leads to Glendale. The moon was big and bright, and it seemed there were more stars than I had ever seen before. As we drove across the barren landscape, I kept my eyes on the moon as it followed us. As if it were moving too. As if the moon was also going to see Papa Joe. As if it had a connection specifically to me. As if the moon knew something. And in its silver glow it seemed to convey a kind of wisdom. A kind of innate and intimate knowledge. Looking at it, concentrating on its illumination, it filled me with peace. Because I was unsettled and I was doing a good job at not letting anyone know, which made it worse.

We were taking our yearly summer trip to Arizona to see Papa Joe and Mary Lou and my other relatives who lived in Glendale. We would stay with Uncle Joshua and his family, and we would visit with my Aunt Carmen and Uncle Ron, at her ranch outside of Glendale. But mostly we were there to see Papa Joe.

Uncle Joshua and Aunt Sharon had a sprawling one-story ranch house with a carport. He had bought it after marrying Sharon, his third wife. Uncle Joshua had three kids. Davey, 13 years old, was his stepson from his first wife, but he had custody of him for whatever reason, even though he was not his natural father. And his daughter Julia, my age, who came from his second wife who had passed away a few years before. And a daughter, Catherine, who was from Joshua and Sharon; she was almost two years old.

Uncle Joshua had dinner for us when we got there. They had already eaten. I voraciously dug into the meatloaf, mashed potatoes, and peas. I hadn't had lunch because I had trouble keeping down food during a long car ride. When I came up for air I noticed Julia, sitting at the other end of the table, not eating, elbows planted on the table, her chin resting on her fists, propped up by her forearms. She was staring at me with a curious smile on her face. I looked at her and flashed my eyes; *what are you looking at?* That made her laugh, and I went back to eating.

My brother and I slept on the floor in the kids' room in sleeping bags that we brought. Julia and Catherine slept in bunk beds, Catherine on the bottom, and Davey had a small bed of his own against the other wall. I didn't mind sleeping on the floor so much; it was hard, but my sleeping bag was soft. I liked sleeping in my sleeping bag, which still smelled of pine needles from when we went camping the summer before. As we lay in the darkness Julia said. "So, what do you guys want to do tomorrow?"

"What is there to do?" Kenny asked playfully.

"Not much," Davey said.

"We can play hide and seek," Catherine offered.

"Sure, we can play hide and seek." Julia said big sisterly.

"Yay!"

"I know something we can do," Davey said.

"Oh no, oh no," Julia cried.

"What?" Kenny asked.

"We can go down to the creek and catch big tree frogs."

"Ew!"

"Um," I said. "I don't know about that."

"Why?" Davey asked incredulously.

"Because it's gross," Julia said.

"Kenny has a thing about them," I said.

"I hate them!" Kenny said, practically shouting.

"Why?" Davey said, sounding genuinely surprised.

It got quiet. "Well," I said. "One night, when we were visiting my Uncle Dan, we were playing tag with my cousins. And Kenny was it, and he was chasing my cousin Darlene, trying to tag her you know, and she ran across their front lawn, Kenny chased after her and he stepped right on top of a one, crushing it, and if that wasn't bad enough he wasn't wearing any shoes, and if that wasn't bad enough when he ran away he crushed another one and if that wasn't bad enough he stepped on another one. I guess the lawn was full of them. When he finally got inside, he went to the bathroom and threw up for a long time. My mom cleaned off all the frog blood and guts from his feet. Ever since then he can't stand them. In fact, he forbade me to even say the word."

"You mean the word…"

"Shut up!" Kenny shouted.

It got quiet again. Finally, Julia said, "We could always just play hide and seek. We have a big backyard, with lots of good places to hide."

"Oh goody," Catherine shouted.

CHAPTER 29

I'm not sure when it started, but somewhere in the middle of the night Catherine woke me up moaning, "I want my daddy, I want my daddy, I want my daddy…" Davey made a big sigh. "Here we go again." It went on for a long time; slowly, progressively getting louder. Eventually she stopped. I went back to sleep.

I was having a dream. Dad was in a boat, in the middle of a lake. I was on the shore, watching him. He saw me and waved. I could see his face even though he was very far away. And then I couldn't see his face. Big, puffy gray clouds began to form in the sky. It started to rain. A bolt of lightning hit his boat. It erupted in flames and then disappeared. I stared at the horizon, not believing my eyes. It stopped raining. The sun came out. And then the boat reappeared. I felt relieved. Then the boat started to sink very slowly. I had no feeling about it.

I was awoken again by Catherine moaning, "I want my daddy…" Sometime towards dawn, Uncle Joshua came in and got her.

The next afternoon, we were playing hide and seek in the backyard; Davey, Kenny, Julia, and myself. After a while it started to rain. Kenny and Davey went inside the house, and Julia and I ran under the carport. We stood there watching the rain. Looking at her I was thinking she didn't look at all like Uncle Joshua; her skin wasn't brown, it was light, and she had blonde hair and a small nose and very long eyelashes. She knew I was looking at her, but she didn't look my way. "I like the rain," she said. "Especially when it is so hot. Does it get this hot in Los Angeles?"

"I don't live in Los Angeles exactly. No. Not this hot."

I knew that she was my cousin. Or was she? Was she by blood or not by blood? Was she Uncle Joshua's daughter or stepdaughter? That missing information mattered a great deal to me at that moment. It was because I wanted to kiss her. This new thing, my new favorite thing was kissing. I thought about how Kathy had asked Man if he wanted to kiss her or me and how he didn't say one way or another. That kind of meant that he did want to kiss me. What would that be like? To kiss a boy. But not just any boy. A very handsome and extraordinary boy. Kathy was pretty, but also tough like a boy. What would be the difference? Julia was more girlish. She said, "The rain is probably hot enough to take a shower in." I laughed. "You don't think so?" She started unbuttoning her pink chiffon blouse. She took it off and dropped it to the ground. She turned to look at me. And then she started to laugh. "You should see your face!" She picked up her blouse and ran into the house.

Julia was sitting at the dining room table drinking a glass of milk when I went back into the house. She had her blouse back on. "You want some milk GG?" Julia said teasingly. I sat down at the table and poured myself a glass of milk from the glass bottle there.

"Where is everyone?" I asked.

"You mean the grownups?"

"Yeah."

"Your mom and dad went to the store or something. My dad is at work and my mom is lying down in the bedroom with Catherine."

"Oh."

"Your brother and Davey are in the living room playing Crazy Eights."

After we finished drinking the milk Julia pointed at me and then turned her hand over and made her forefinger curl back and forth. I shrugged, stood up and went over to her. She led me through the living room. We passed Davey and Kenny sitting on the floor playing cards. They didn't seem to register our presence. She took me to a big piano at the far corner of the room. She sat down at the piano bench. "Do you want to hear me play piano?" I nodded dumbly. "First close your eyes." I did as instructed. "Now, just stand there." I heard her rustling around with some papers. I figured that she was getting some sheet music out. I took lessons for a while, but I hated it and so begged for my parents to let me stop.

She started playing the piano. I recognized the music. She was playing the music from the movie The Sting, which I had seen earlier in the summer. Cousin Cassandra had taken me and my brother. She made us promise to tell my parents that she took us to see the Apple Dumpling Gang instead. She just had to see every movie that Robert Redford made. There was just something inexplicable about him for her, a thing she called sex appeal. Something that made her want to completely forget her life and everyone in it. Paul Newman had *it* too.

Julia was playing the main song from the movie, and she sounded just great. I couldn't believe she could play the piano so well. The music sounded just like in the movie. And then she said, "Okay, you can open your eyes now." I opened my eyes and looked down at her, she was making her hands practically dance on the piano keys. It was amazing! She stood up but the piano kept playing the music. She started to laugh. The boys on the floor started laughing too. She opened two sliding doors on the front of the piano and pointed to where there was a paper roll with little holes spinning on two wheels. "You should see your face!"

CHAPTER 30

After lunch we went to see Papa Joe. Julia rode in our car and Kenny rode with Uncle Joshua and his family. I noticed it had stopped raining. Julia grabbed my arm and said, "Hey, look! It's the most incredible thing!" She stretched her other arm over my body and pointed out my window. And there was the most vast, dense, startlingly defined rainbow I had ever seen. The gradient colors vibrating against a sharp blue sky. I had only recently read about the construction of rainbows in one of my brother's National Geographic magazines; how it is composed of a trillion tiny raindrops that the sun filters through. But to see one, one that looked like a painting, was another matter.

Julia knew even more than I did about rainbows. "Razzmic Berry, is the purple foundation. Razzmic, I love that word! Wide and seemingly strong enough to hold the thing up in the sky. So luscious that you want to eat it. The Razzmic Berry blends into a blue stripe. Blue turning green turning yellow. Yellow, the belt of the rainbow, called Gargoyle Gas, the lifeline of the rainbow, the central most vibrant color, the color that plays on fantasy and desire, the part of the rainbow that speaks to wish fulfillment. Then comes Sunset Orange, which harkens back to the theme of time's translucent and temporary quality. Really the whole point of a rainbow. And at the top a very thin and transparent strip of Button Blue which quickly melds into an azure sky."

I was more amazed by Julia's explanation of the rainbow than the rainbow itself.

"What's wrong with you?" Julia said to me. "Your mouth is hanging open."

"Where did you learn all of that?"

"A place called the public library," she said tauntingly.

"Let's go find the pot of gold," I exclaimed.

"Well," my father said, "it looks like the pot of gold just might be at Papa Joe's house. That's where it appears the end of the rainbow is landing."

We pulled into Papa Joe's driveway. Uncle Joshua right behind us in his Volkswagen van. As everyone piled out of the cars, Davey cried, "Did you see that rainbow!?"

Papa Joe lived in a house he built in the 1920's. Same house my mom and all of her brothers and sisters grew up in. It was made of construction blocks painted white, a roof made of curved orange clay tiles and a floor which was a slab of concrete painted burnt sienna. All that concrete helped keep the house cool on hot summer days. In the front yard, which was just dirt and rocks, stood a big old Emory Oak tree, perfect for climbing and perching. From it you could watch the big trucks go by. The backyard was an adventure in and of itself. I couldn't wait to go and explore. But first we had to visit with Papa Joe and have lunch. Which was all right.

Papa Joe had an otherworldly stature in our family. Like a saint that looked like Buddha. He sat in his big Naugahyde recliner chair. All the children climbed up on his lap like he was Santa Claus. He wouldn't or didn't speak much English, but he would ask how we were: "How is school? Chico." Either Chico or Chica depending on the kid. And he would laugh, an elegant, tickled laugh, the sound of which emanated from the back of his mouth, you could see the silver over his molars, and he had a full set of clean white teeth, and beautiful breath, like papayas, and a great shock of black and silver hair on the top of his head. "Papa Joe, let me see your thumb!" The thumb on his left hand had been decapitated. He would show us and laugh. I was fascinated by Papa Joe's thumb. Or half a thumb. And he liked showing it off.

Sitting on his lap, reclining three quarters of the way. He would show it to us, the stump. Smooth at the top, like an anthropomorphized bald person. "An electric saw," he said. "Just like that," he said. "Always be careful with electric things," he said. And laughed. Changing the subject, he reminded us that, "I knew Geronimo the bandit, when he was old and was performing in carnivals." He sneezed and blew his nose into a red bandana that he quickly pulled from his back pocket. "I was just a kid, the same age as you. I had heard that Geronimo hated Mexicans and had even killed a great many of them. But he was nice to me. He was most famous for killing white people. That's what he was famous for."

Mary Lou, who wasn't his wife, and maybe was his girlfriend, was always present and quite jovial. She made tamales from scratch. When Dad said that they were the best tamales in the world, this would make Mary Lou embarrassed, and she laughed in denial. And I thought they were pretty good too. But I liked the way she made rice even better. Yellow rice with bits of sweet tomatoes.

After lunch, Davey, Kenny, Julia, and I went out back. My mother told us to be careful, that we never knew what we would find out there. "Don't worry," Dad chuckled, "They have had their tetanus shots." In the backyard, there were rows of homemade shelves, filled with every possible thing that might interest a boy. Or a girl like Julia. A museum of relics, like stepping into past times. There were axes and saws and buckets of rusty nails and old leather suitcases with straps, and steamer trunks, and broken electric fans and random parts from cars, broken record players and radios, and army stuff, like canteens and helmets and shovels that folded over at the top: painted on the side- U.S. ARMY.

"Hey! Look what I found," shouted Billy from the inside of a little tin shack. We all went to the shack. You had to knock the cobwebs from your face as you entered. There, inside were shelves filled with coffee canisters and jars most of which were labeled with two XX's. Davey was holding what looked to be a metal belt that had a long chain attached to it and connected to its other end was some sort of clasp. "What is it?" I asked.

Davey looked at each one of us and said, "This belt, this belt was made for prisoners so that they can't get away. Probably very dangerous ones like murderers. See, there's a place to put a lock around the belt and a place to put a lock at the end of the chain which goes around the foot." We all looked at it in wonder. "What's Papa Joe doing with it?" Julia asked. "Ah, you know Papa Joe, he just picks up all sorts of things." Davey looked at each one of us and said, "Who wants to try it on?" We looked at each other. "No way!" Julia cried. "What about you GG?" I shook my head. "Ah come one. Nothing to be afraid of. I don't even have the locks." I thought about it. I was scared but I knew that there was nothing to be afraid of. Not really. And I wanted to show everyone that I was no scaredy cat. "Okay. I'll try it on."

"Help me out Julia. I'll put the belt around his waist, and you put the clasp around his ankle." Julia nodded. Davey reached around me and before I knew it, he had slipped a lock around the belt, locked it and then quickly got down on his knees and put a lock through the clasp. "Hey!" I shouted, "What are you doing?" Davey and Kenny laughed. Julia begrudgingly joined them in laughter. I felt anxious to be trapped by this big heavy thing. To be trapped like an animal. To be stripped of all human dignity. I was about to cry when without any movement of my own volition the belt fell to the ground. "Ah. Why do you have to be so skinny?" Davey said. "I'm going to tell!" I whimpered. Sensing that I was going to cry for real, he pulled from his pocket a skeleton key and unlocked the lock around my foot. I wiped the tears from my eyes with my shirt sleeve. I looked at the kids, and then I started to laugh too.

CHAPTER 31

Aunt Carmen was the de-facto matriarch of the family. She had dyed black hair; the style was as if it were 1944, long in back and cut in a line above the eyes. She wore flowing floral print dresses, crimson lipstick and big glasses with coke bottle lenses. And she had a booming and often intimidating voice. Her accent was strong and her laugh loud and frequent. She and Uncle Ron lived on a ranch at the foot of the Hedgepeth Hills in a house that Aunt Carmen had designed, and that Uncle Ron had built practically single handedly. He was this very well built, handsome man who was at the absolute beck and call of Aunt Carmen. And he seemed to love it. Whenever she asked him to do something she called him, Lover. "Build me a house Lover." And he never hesitated. I never saw him cross. Always a placid smile fixed to his face.

The house was unlike any house that I had ever seen. A two-story structure, part brick and part adobe, the back half of the second story built on a cantilever, held up by two large steel poles. There was a separate structure, a large space with a flat roof, that served as his workshop. They called it a ranch, but it didn't seem like they were raising any livestock or anything for that matter. They had a pen which they kept goats. They had two goats the summer before, but the coyotes got them. So, they got two more. In fact, every time we came to visit, Aunt Carmen would have a new set of animals. And every time those animals would be replaced by another set because of the coyotes. She loved to pick up strays. Kittens, dogs, puppies but they all were inevitably slaughtered or carried off by the coyotes, or bobcats and sometimes mountain lions. All except Boy, her little Lhasa Apso, the most unpleasant dog I had ever encountered. If anyone came near the beast, let alone try to pet it, it made a sound which was a cross between a yap and a growl and would spring forth snapping. I made the mistake once of trying to pet Boy and was left with a terribly painful puncture mark on my hand. You can still see the little dots.

At dinner time Aunt Carmen had designated a table for the kids just outside the dining room on the patio. She liked to segregate the kids for meals. She didn't dislike children, though she never had any of her own, she just had trouble tolerating children's voices. Something about the sound of it caused her to have a headache. Or so she said. But we were just outside the patio door. Within earshot of the adult table.

Before we could eat, we would have to wait until Papa Joe said the prayer. Which was lengthy and in Spanish. When it seemed that he had concluded the prayer, we, the kids, would grab for our forks, only to realize that we were premature, he was only taking a breather. Sitting down for dinner I would think that perhaps I didn't have much of an appetite because of the pre-dinner snacking on Mexican cinnamon and sugar cookies; only to be ravenous by the time Papa Joe finished his prayer. That glorious "Amen" was one of the most wonderful words in any language.

Aunt Carmen told the story of Papa Joe coming to America, a story we had heard many times before: "Pancho Villa was rounding up all the boys in all the villages and towns to join the fight in his revolution. Papa Joe lived in Nogales with his mom, two sisters, and an older brother. Pancho Villa's army got his older brother, or his older brother joined voluntarily, no one can remember. Well, he was killed fighting the government forces. Grandma did not want that same fate to befall little Joe. He was only ten years old, but she knew that it was just a matter of time. She put him on a train to live with relatives here in Glendale. That was 1910. Arizona had just become a state in America. Before then it was Mexico. Then the relatives all died of influenza in 1918, but by then he was old enough to take care of himself. He started his own construction business and did darn good. He never saw his mama or his sisters again. But they stayed in touch by letters, which are in a shoebox underneath his bed. Isn't that right, Papa?" She nodded at him, and he just smiled. But I saw that there were tears in his eyes.

CHAPTER 32

Papa Joe and Mary Lou left not long after dinner. Uncle Joshua took them home. "Papa Joe doesn't like being at Aunt Carmen's after dark," Mom told me. "Why?" I asked. She shrugged her shoulders. The other kids went off to play but I stayed and listened to the adults talk. Aunt Carmen was grilling my father. They always had the same conversation. It seemed like a routine.

"How can you tell me that you don't believe in God?"

My father, finishing his third serving of sopapillas, replied. "Easy. It makes no sense to me. You have faith. Okay. I respect that. I just can't make that leap of faith in an idea that makes no sense to me."

"How can you live like that? Is there no meaning in the world for you?"

"Of course, there's meaning."

"You don't believe in Jesus Christ?"

"No. No, I don't. There is no proof that there was Jesus. A Jesus Christ. The people who wrote the bible were not even alive when Jesus was supposed to have lived."

Carmen gasped. "You know what that means—you're going to hell. Simple as that. You don't have faith and if you don't have faith, you have no grace. Yes, it saddens me to say it, it really does, but you are definitely going to hell."

"Hell and heaven, those are just ideas made up to keep people in line. Crowd control. But I feel there is an inherent sense of right and wrong without religion collecting revenue to pay for it. Religion is just big business. For instance, even without religion, people know that killing, stealing, lying are wrong. And they know they will pay the price that society has implemented. Behaving morally has nothing to do with religion. On the other hand, people who say they are Christian, have no problem going to war and killing innocent civilians, women, and children. Richard Nixon is a Christian, he is a Quaker; whose main tenet is a refusal to participate in war, and yet he has no problem napalming villages inhabited by women and children. No disrespect, Ron."

Uncle Ron was a very nice man. You couldn't deny it. He looked like Richard Widmark in horn rim glasses. He had hardly ever spoke and he had a sweet, gentle smile. He had served in the Air Force, fought in Vietnam and probably personally dropped a ton of napalm. But he just smiled at my father's words. "No disrespect taken." And yet, if what Dad was saying was true, and it seemed to be judging from the photos that I had seen, then Uncle Ron had committed terrible crimes against innocent civilians. How could we sit there having dinner with him? He was basically a mass murderer. And yet he was my uncle, a genuinely nice man. Always very kind to me.

Julia again asked me to come and play, I told her that I was still eating dessert. I was very interested in what the grownups were talking about. It seemed almost completely arbitrary as to who was a good person and who was a bad person. At least how the world looked at it. One person kills many people, and they are given medals and awards. Another person like Mr. Pacheco kills his own wife and nothing happens to him. And yet the best people, the kindest people, like my mom, well, nobody gives them any medals or awards. Uncle Joshua walked in from taking Papa Joe home. He too had served in the Air Force in Vietnam, and he wasn't so quiet as Uncle Ron. "What we were doing in Vietnam was trying to stop communism in its tracks. Because if the communists infiltrate that entire region, it is just a matter of time before it spreads to our shores. Look at the hippies. And we could have won."

"Well, we lost Vietnam. Because the Vietnamese wanted to decide how to run their own government and were willing to die for it by the hundreds of thousands. And as a result, tens of thousands of American soldiers were…"

Just then my mom came into the room from the kitchen where she and Aunt Sharon were doing the dishes. She put her hands on my father's shoulders, which he knew indicated that he was to stop talking, immediately. She said, "There is a thing called a conscience, everyone has one, they were born with one. Whether they choose to use it is another story. But I think we can stop talking about unpleasant things now." The faces around the table were flushed, but, again, it wasn't the first time that they had had this conversation; it occurred every summer when we came to visit. And my aunt and uncle never seemed to hold resentment against my father for his opinions. They were always nice to him. But my Aunt Carmen once said to me, "You better receive Jesus Christ as your personal savior, because you don't want to burn in hell for eternity like your father."

Man wore a cross around his neck, but I never asked him about it. I had seen a lot of movies about Jesus on TV, and about the Bible. My favorite being the Ten Commandments, because in that one Moses had superpowers. More than any Marvel Comics book hero, *they* had never parted the waters of an ocean. That movie was on TV every Easter. And The Greatest Story Ever Told, this one had Charlton Heston too, only he didn't play Jesus, he played John the Baptist, and he had his head removed. In both these movies, there was so much terribleness unleashed on the world, and it didn't seem like God or Jesus could do or did anything to stop it from happening—plagues, diseases, persecution, the killing of every newborn child by King Herod, murder, slavery, burning hail, rivers of blood, orgies. Nothing like that happens in a Marvel Comic.

But I was fascinated by this Jesus man. And how despite

everything that my dad said, people still believed in all of what Dad called nonsense. And he was right in that the same people who called themselves Christian were the same people who thought that the Vietnam War was righteous. It didn't make sense, but their conversation got me thinking about that cross around Man's neck. Such a gruesome thing when you think about it. Around your neck, on a little cross, the depiction of a man slowly dying. Not dying from the wounds to his hands and feet, as gruesome as they are, but he dies slowly, by suffocating. And every day you put that around your neck?

CHAPTER 33

Aunt Carmen gave us a bucket full of carrots, corncobs and celery to give to the goats. At first, timidly, we reached our hands through the fence, taking turns feeding the animals. But once we got used to the way they went after the food and not our fingers we became more self-assured. The goats lurched and blew air through their noses this made me and Julia giggle. "Guess these guys will be gone next time we visit," Kenny said. "Yep. Sure thing," Davey laughed. "Why does she do it, I mean, shouldn't she have a better fence, or something," Julia said sitting on the top part of the simple two board fence. Gesturing with his hands to the large expanse before us, Davey said, "Remember those two Mexican Hairless dogs she had two summers ago?" We nodded our heads. "Well, I was here on the night they were taken by the coyotes, what a terrible, terrible sound. It was around this time at night, and I was in Uncle Ron's workshop playing around and then I heard the sounds; screeching, howling, crying sounds of the kill, the sounds of the pack of coyotes, all vicious and growling as they tore apart the dogs. In some ways it sounded like humans fighting. And I ran out here and there was blood everywhere. And the coyotes running off with the carcasses. I think that Aunt Carmen, I don't know, maybe she likes feeding the coyotes."

"Is that what you think?" It was Aunt Carmen. She seemed to appear out of nowhere. Standing there with Boy cradled in her arms. "You think I like feeding my expensive Xoloitzcuintles to the coyotes?" You could practically hear

Davey gulp. "Well, I don't! That is not my intention." Her coke bottle glasses had slipped to the bridge of her nose. With the hand holding Boy's bottom she pushed them up, turning Boy upside down. "But if the coyotes didn't eat certain animals, then they would maybe attack us humans."

Talking very slowly and deliberately she went on. "You see, the coyotes here are not just coyotes. They are possessed. Do you know what possesses them?" "The devil?" Julia said, sounding a little snide. "No! Julia. The dead. The dead possess this land, and the dead possess the coyotes." She looked at each one of us, gathering up our frightened faces with her eyes. "You see. Many years ago, the church owned this land, and they used it to hide the refugees fleeing the violence in Mexico. Many of them were Yaqui Indians who had been sold into slavery to work on the sugar plantations in Oaxaca and Yucatan. The church had to keep the refugees hidden because the vigilantes were doing a mass deportation. Even for those who had become citizens." "What's deportation?" Davey asked. "Deportation is when they take people, forcibly, and make them go back to their old country. One day they came to take a man who owned land near here. He fought back, and one of the white men was killed. The next day they killed the man and his family and burned down his ranch. Then they came to the refugee camp, which was right here, on this land, and they slaughtered everyone. Man, woman, and child. It was called the Hora de Sangre, The Hour of Blood. If you put your ear to the ground, you can hear lurking the spirits of the Yaqui migrants who never got baptized. They are forever trapped in purgatory. Your grandma was trying to get all of them baptized when she caught TB and died. And you, who have not been baptized, will go and be trapped in purgatory unless you accept Jesus. Unless you get baptized." I knew she was talking about me and my brother. "So, when the coyotes get fed, the spirits have peace for a short while." She had accomplished her goal of frightening us. "This is the truth. I am telling you." And she turned and went back inside. After we were sure that she was gone we got down on all fours and put our ears to the ground. "Do you hear anything," I asked Julia. She closed her eyes. I closed my eyes too and I could have sworn that I heard a baby crying.

We were going to camp out that night in pup tents, under the starry night on the mesa. My parents went home with Uncle Joshua and Aunt Sharon. They would pick us up in the morning. We went through the process of setting up the tents in the open area behind the back of the house. Davey, holding a Coleman lamp, put it to his face and said, "I'm the ghost of the victims of the Hedgepath Hill massacre." Julia punched him in the arm. "Stop that Davey. But no kidding, I don't believe in ghosts, but I do believe in coyotes. We're crazy to sleep out here." At last, someone was making sense. "Julia's right," I said. "There's no way…" Davey interrupted me. "What are you? Chicken?"

"Well, they kind of have a point," Kenny said.

"Kind of have of point? I'm going inside. I don't care, I'll sleep on the kitchen floor." Julia said.

"Okay, okay," Davey interjected, "We could bring our sleeping bags to the roof of Uncle Ron's workshop. No way coyotes can get up there. I slept up there once last summer. Aunt Carmen said it was ok."

We all agreed it was the best thing to do. Davey got a double extension ladder from inside the garage, leaned it against the side of the wall of the workshop and we all climbed up. After unrolling my sleeping bag, I laid down upon it. It was not very comfortable as there were little pebbles on the roof. But I was distracted from that by the vast night's sky. The sky was absolutely filled up with light. It was so bright you could practically read a book by the starlight.

I put my sleeping bag next to Julia. We laid there on our backs identifying stars, planets, and constellations. I knew a fair amount about astronomy, having gotten interested in the NASA space program and Skylab. But Julia knew even more.

Kenny and Davey were playing Crazy 8's not paying any attention to us or the stars.

"What's your favorite constellation?" she asked.

"I guess Orion, maybe because it was the first one, I recognized. Also, in Cypress we don't have as many stars, but I can always see that one."

"Everyone likes Ursa Major or Ursa Minor, The Big Dipper, but I think I like Lyra best. Tucked away in the corner of the sky."

I hadn't heard of that one. "Why is it called Lyra?"

"Well, the story goes, Orpheus was given a harp from Apollo, and the music that he made on the lyre, that's what they called a harp in those days, and when Orpheus played it, it was the most beautiful music in the whole world. If you were angry it would make your anger go away, or if you were sad it would make you happy. He was able to charm rocks and streams with his music, just the most beautiful music. And he loved to play it for his wife Eurydice. Who loved to hear it. And they loved each other very much. One day Eurydice was wandering in a field. A shepherd saw her. He thought that she was the most beautiful woman that he had ever seen. But Eurydice loved Orpheus and wouldn't pay the shepherd any mind. The shepherd chased her, and she tripped on a rock and a snake bit her, and she died."

"I saw a rattlesnake the other day," Davey said. Apparently listening in on our conversation.

"Really?" Kenny asked. "Where?"

"Just on the side of the road. You see them all the time around here."

"What did you do?"

"What do you think I did? I ran away!" They both laughed.

"Anyway! Eurydice died and Orpheus was so sad that he stopped praying to the Gods. Which made Dionysus so angry he sent his followers to tear Orpheus limb from limb and throw his harp in the river Hebrus. Which was just as well because after he died Zeus sent Orpheus to spend eternity with Eurydice in Hades. And Jupiter took the Lyra from the river and then threw it up into the sky which is where it is to this day."

"How do you know all of that?" Kenny asked. Amazed that a girl was so smart.

"I told you, I read books."

CHAPTER 34

I had trouble sleeping. Everything that Aunt Carmen had said about the coyotes and the Hora de Sangre disturbed me. I wondered why people had a need or were compelled to do such violence. Even to children. What kind of person massacres a camp of people like they did at Hedgepath Hill? I wanted to ask Julia. Seems like she knew a lot of things, maybe she had an answer for that. "Psst. Julia." No answer. "Pssst, Julia." Again, no answer. I got out of my sleeping bag and crawled over to hers. She was not there. I looked over to where my brother and Davey's sleeping bags were; they were there, asleep. I stood and walked to the edge of the roof. I saw Julia sitting on the fence where the goats were kept.

I climbed down from the roof and walked over to her. "Hey." I said. She didn't respond.

I tapped her on the shoulder, and she fell off the fence. I helped her up. "Oh my god! You scared the bejeezus out of me!" After she calmed down, I asked her, "What are you doing?"

"What do you think I'm doing? I'm waiting for the coyotes."

"Aren't you scared?"

"Of what?"

"That they'll get you!"

"That's why."

"That's why what?"

"I like to be scared. It makes you feel alive."

"But if they get you, you won't be alive."

"That's what makes it exciting."

"You're crazy!"

"Well, nobody's making you stay. Besides, they don't want me. They want the goats."

And yet, I couldn't move. It's not that I wanted to wait for the coyotes, or that I wanted to see the coyotes attack the goats. I just felt better to be near Julia than to be up on the roof. We both climbed back on the fence.

"Julia?"

"Yeah?"

"That stuff, that Aunt Carmen was saying. Do you think it's true?

"Which part?

"The part about those white people coming and killing all the people who lived here. The children too."

"Of course, that happened. Or stuff like it. All that other stuff is just folk tales. Aunt Carmen is a little crazy."

"How could people do that?"

"Not people. Men. Men did that."

"But how could they?"

"Well, it's like the coyotes. It's not just one coyote that comes and attacks the goats or whatever animal Aunt Carmen leaves for sacrifice. It's a pack. It has to be a pack. And it's just like that for men. I mean what is war? It's just packs of men doing violence."

"Yeah. I guess so."

We stayed on the fence for a while, watching the goats who were down on the ground, resting against each other. One of the goats had his head down while the other had his head up and eyes open. "One sleeps while the other keeps watch. They take turns," Julia said. After a while I could barely keep my eyes open. Julia climbed down from the fence. "Come on. Let's be like the goats. One of us sleeps while the other watches. And we'll take turns. Okay?" Yawning, I said, "Okay." She gave me a little smile, patted me on the back and said, "I'll take the first shift."

I was on the desert. Standing motionless. Just rocks and sand, a blazing sun in the sky and me. About ten in front of me was a boy and a woman with their backs turned. He was dressed in a black suit and the woman was dressed in a long white dress. There was a strange cloud around them, a gray and white cloud encircling them. I walked up to them. As I approached, they turned round. It was Man and his mom. Only their faces were green. She opened the top of her dress with her hands to reveal her beating heart. He held a baseball bat that was covered in blood. He smiled, he seemed glad to see me. The only thing was his eyes were gone and there was blood dripping from them. I thought, I know this story. The mother's face turned from a happy expression to a terrified expression. I heard moaning. I looked at my feet. There was Hector. He died just as I said his name. Man pushed his mother to the ground and stood over her. I heard an animal growling, screaming, howling. I quickly turned around. It was Man's father. He was howling like a coyote, and his head was bleeding profusely. He was holding the same baseball bat that Man had been holding only seconds before. He raised it and slammed it down on my head. I fell to the ground. He tossed the bat and climbed on top of me and let out another horrible sound. He grabbed me by the shoulders and started shaking me. I looked to Man for help, but he just stood there frozen. I let out a scream. Man's father started laughing.

And there was more laughing. Somebody called my name, "G.G.!" I turned and it was Julia. She was angry. We were where we had fallen asleep. It was morning. "You jerks!" Julia spat at Kenny and Davey. They were laughing hysterically. "Ha ha! We scared the heck out of you guys!" Davey said. Kenny pointed to my short pants, "Did you pee your pants, Gerald?" I looked down. And I had. Davey said, chuckling, "Oh, I'm sorry, did you guys think we were coyotes or something?" Julia came up to him and slapped him hard across the face. Davey looked like he was going to spring at her, but Kenny stepped in and held him back. "You're not my Daddy!" Davey shouted. Julia started to cry. I guessed that was something that she didn't do very often. Davey calmed himself. "Come on. Let's go in. You better change your pants G.G." I took off running. I made for Hedgepath Hill.

CHAPTER 35

I heard them call my name, but I kept running. I went over the lower side of the hill down into a wooded area where there was a mix of cacti and mulberry trees. The sun's light was breaking through the brush. It was very green and lush. It seemed like I had entered another land altogether. I wondered for a second if I was still dreaming.

It was already getting hot. I came to a pass where there was a herd of cattle. Which I found odd. Odd upon odd. They didn't seem like the kind of cows I had seen before. There was something foreboding about them. The way they looked at me in unison. Something almost human about them. But they looked just like cows. Cows staring at me. They frightened me. I started to sing a made-up melody, no words. I thought this might keep the cows at bay. I had never heard of cows attacking people but still I was scared. I then thought that I needed to confront my fears and so I walked to the one that was at the front of the herd. Very slowly. And when I got close enough, I very gently put my arms around its neck. I hugged the animal singing softly in its ear. It shifted its weight. Still, I held it. The cow let out a big sigh. I felt that it was at peace. From the back of the herd came another sound, like a man yelling "God!". The whole herd started to make noise and shift. I ran away. I tripped and fell into some prickly pears. My arms and face got all scratched up. I got to my feet and looked behind me. But the cows hadn't moved from where they were.

I walked very quietly until I left the grove and passed into another more open area.

I was getting so hot I thought I might pass out. And I didn't know if I was lost. I knew I could turn back and follow the path that led me to where I was, follow it back. But I didn't want to. I felt the need to keep moving forward. I knew that when I wanted to head back, if I walked perpendicular to the side of the hill, I could go up and over to the foot of the hill and there find my aunt's ranch. The brush was getting denser. I had never seen land like this in Arizona. Bushes with yellow flowers that looked like bells, shrubs with purple flowers and butterflies dancing on and near the petals, tumbleweeds, prickly pears, barrel cacti, rocks that looked like faces; in my state of dehydration, I was overwhelmed. I sat down on a large rock. Unable to go any further.

I sat on the rock and looked all around me. It was as if I was sitting on a sculpture in the middle of a great empty town. I closed my eyes halfway and everything became patterns and shapes and colors. I got dizzy and weird in the head. And everything became hazier. I saw little sparks of yellow light. I got frightened again. I got up and jumped up and down and fell to the ground. When I got up, I was so glad that everything had definition again. I was so glad that I started to dance. I danced to the songs that came into my head.

I went on, creeping through the bushes. I brushed against some standing nettle, it stung my bare legs, but I didn't mind. It only made me laugh. I thought about what Julia told me about being afraid of being killed by the coyotes, how it made her feel more alive. The scratches from the prickly pear on my arms and face and now the stinging from the nettle on my legs only made me feel more alive.

I came upon a circular wall of green stones. The opening was about six feet in circumference which protruded about two feet off the ground. I went to it. A great well filled with sparkling blue water, with dense green moss all over the edges of the opening. I leaned over the wall and stuck my head into the water. Lifted my head out and shook off the water. Then I bent down into it, put my lips on the surface of the water, like I was kissing the water, and then I opened my mouth and sucked the water up. It tasted unlike any water that I had ever had. But it tasted like what water should taste like. In Southern California the water had a lot of different things that they put into it. This tasted pure and by drinking it I felt I was having a pure connection to God.

I took off all my clothes. I dunked my shorts and underwear in the water to wash off the pee and then I put them on a rock to dry. I got into the well. The water felt soft and cool. I was curious as to how deep it was. I submerged myself but couldn't hold my breath long enough to hit the bottom. As I came up nearer to the surface of the water, I saw these strange little fish. Or were they bugs? They were oval lengthwise and perfectly round. About the size of a quarter. These too had a human quality; only they were undeniably friendly. They seemed to be interested in me. They came up and brushed against me in a sweet and gentle way. It tickled. They had big eyes. And little wings or fins that fluttered from their sides. They seemed to be very curious as to who this creature was who had come into their habitat. With every movement I made they followed me. I never wanted to leave. But then I remembered that my father and mother were coming back to pick me and my brother up. My mother would be very worried that I had gone missing.

When I got out of the water, I noticed that the marks from the prickly pear and the scratches from the nettle were gone. I put on my clothes, which had dried, and headed for the route that I had mapped out in my head. Emerging from the brush and into the open, dry and barren land on the side of the hill; the sun came down hard on me, but I had been refreshed by the well. The sun's intense heat felt preternaturally enlivening.

I was thinking about how I would tell Julia about those strange creatures I had seen in the well, and the foreboding cattle. We would laugh about these things. Julia had come to my defense. She had taught me so much about the stars. She was truly a good person. I knew this. She might even be somebody I could talk to about some of the things that had been happening to me. It would feel good to talk about them. To somebody. I could tell her about Man. About what happened to his mother at the hands of his father. How he was such a sweet boy. A genuinely nice boy. How could such terrible things happen to such a nice boy? Maybe Julia had a good idea about it.

Then I heard a buzzing sound and looked down to see a coiled rattlesnake about three feet away from me. It lifted its head, and it showed its fangs. I jumped straight up into the air, came down and started running. I slipped on a rock and skinned my knee. Got back up and kept running even after I was clear of the rattlesnake. When I finally felt safe enough to catch my breath I stopped running. I noticed that all the scratches from the prickly pear and nettle had returned.

CHAPTER 36

What happened to you!" Kenny shouted. Mom put down the phone and came running to me. She embraced me tightly and said angrily, "Where have you been?" I tried to speak but nothing came out except for tears. Later, in the quiet of the bathroom, as Mom was nursing my wounds, applying Bactine to my scratches, which hurt worse than incurring the scratches, and then as she put a Band-Aid on my knee, she asked me again. I told her what Aunt Carmen had said about the dead from the "Hour of Blood" possessing the coyotes, and how if you put your ear on the ground, you could hear the victims moaning. The ones who hadn't been baptized. And how Julia and I slept outside to protect the goats from the coyotes but fell asleep. And the nightmare- without giving much detail. And how Kenny and Davey pretended they were coyotes attacking to scare us awake. And how I peed my pants.

"Oh, well. I see." She kissed the band aid and then my forehead. "You know. I love my sister but there are many things that we don't agree about. She tends to try to scare people into believing the things that she believes. That wasn't right for Kenny and Davey to do that, or for Kenny to make fun of you. I know that you are sensitive about that. But you aren't old enough to run off by yourself."

One morning, a few years back when I was seven years old, after we had spent the night at my grandparents' house in Downey, I peed the bed. Which was something that I occasionally did until I was eight years old. I sat on a chair, in my underwear watching as my grandmother stripped the sheets off and took them into the laundry. I was getting my clothes on when my grandfather and my brother came into the room and started to chastise me about wetting the bed. "I thought you were a kid, but maybe you're still a baby. Because only babies wet the bed," Grandpa said. "Yeah," Kenny chimed in. I ran out of the room in tears to my mother's arms. A little later she had terse words with my grandfather.

It seemed like I was always taking refuge in my mother's arms. And it seemed like my brother and maybe even my father resented our bond.

CHAPTER 37

Through the screen door his face looked dark and grainy, like an old black and white photo; someone out of the past, not like a boy but like an old, old man.

"Hi Man. How is everything?"

"Terrible," he said, his face a holograph.

"What's wrong?".

He looked at me and laughed an odd laugh, a kind of hissing really, and he said in a quiet voice, "What's wrong? Everything." And in a whisper. "He knows that I know. I know he does. And what's worse is, he knows that you know."

"Let's go for a bike ride."

"Okay."

He opened the screen door and stepped out into the sunlight. He was no longer an old man but a young kid. His eyes were bright, and his face had a confident demeanor that I had not seen before. But it wasn't confidence, it was more a kind of peaceful resignation to what was bound to be something violent and ugly to come.

We rode to the park and sat on the grass. "How do you know that he knows?"

"Well, he asked me if I had been talking to you about kissing girls. And we had only talked about it in my room that one time, and how could he know that? And he said that you were a good kid, a smart kid, and he could see why I would want to be friends with you, but if I thought that I knew something, then he wouldn't stop, he wouldn't hesitate in preventing a betrayal." He looked down at his feet, noticed his shoe was untied and tied it. Then he looked up at the sky, took a breath and said, "Yes. I am quite sure. He knows that I know certain things, and he knows that I don't have many friends, but you are a friend, the kind of friend he had never seen me have before—that is, except for Hector."

"But we weren't in your room when we talked about kissing. We were here."

"Oh. Maybe he read my poems."

"You wrote poems about what we talk about?"

"They are all metaphorical, what is called allegorical poetry. The meaning of the poems is buried behind ideas, things opposite to their true meaning, buried behind walls made of sights and smells and religious figures. My mother taught me about it. She used to do it all the time. But I hide my notebooks. I hide them good. I don't think he could have found them."

"Oh Man. That's probably how he knows things. Where are they now?"

"I destroyed them. I won't write anymore. I'm done."

"So, does he think— does he know that you know for sure? And does he think that you told me and Hector?"

"I don't know. But the thing is, Hector is dead."

"Hector is dead?"

"Yes. He was killed by a hit and run driver. He was riding his bike home from visiting me. Hector lived in Long Beach, where we used to live. The sun was going down, it was getting dark, and the weird thing; the person that hit him was a cop that my father used to work with, who had been put on leave from the force for doing drugs. They found his car with blood on it, and they found him in his living room, zonked out on drugs."

I put my hand over my mouth. I was so utterly shocked by this news. I liked Hector. He was a nice kid, and he had something special about him. Something I couldn't identify but something that set him apart. I had never known any kids who had died. The news of his death had so much significance, so reverberated in my chest, that I couldn't understand it. Like taking a bite of a piece of steak, only it's too big for you to swallow so you must spit it out. But Man seemed detached from it.

Looking straight away, he said, "You should probably stop hanging out with me."

"Why?"

"Why? Because. My dad."

"I'm not afraid of him."

"You should be."

"You think that your dad killed Hector?"

"I don't know. The cop whose car it was hated my father. I know that. I heard them arguing one day, after my mom died. The guy was really angry, maybe he was drunk, I don't know, but he said that my dad was a monster"

"He could have been drunk driving when he hit Hector. After all, he was in trouble for that kind of thing."

"Yeah. Could have. Still. He is right about my father being a monster. The kind of monster that doesn't show any emotion. He doesn't even get angry. When he hits me, you never see it coming. Because he doesn't show emotion. He never showed any sign of feeling bad about killing my mom. That's why he is a monster. And the worst kind."

"We need to do something. We need to—you need to tell someone what you saw. I bet there are already people who suspect something. Like that cop. Nobody ever gets away with murder."

"Cops do. All the time."

I asked Man how he had heard about Hector's death. He said that his father had told him. Had told him in a gentle way. He was compassionate in a way he had never been before. And he put his arm around Man, which he never did, and then asked Man if he wanted to cry. But Man revealed no emotion to his father. Now it was his turn. And, for all his compassion and empathy, just like everything with Mr. Pacheco, there was an underlying threat of violence.

After Man told me all of this, he said we should go home.

And we rode our bikes back to his house. Stopping at the driveway he said, "Just be careful. Don't tell anyone what you know about me, about me and my mom. Just don't talk." He walked his bike to the side of his house, parked it, and went inside.

CHAPTER 38

I got home; Kenny almost ran into me running out the door. "Hey, you got to come, and see?"

"See what?" I asked.

"Greg Gibson is going to blow up a trash can."

Greg Gibson had a chemistry lab in his garage. His father was a scientist, and had brought him microscopes, beakers, chemicals, and compounds. We had seen him use certain combinations of chemicals to dissolve bugs, make smoke bombs, and blow-up model airplanes. But a trash can?

We all met in the parking lot behind the Tastee Freeze. At first, I thought he was going to blow up one of those big green metal trash cans, but then I saw him pull out a regular metal trash can that was by the back door of the pet store. He poured the contents of it into another trash can and pulled it out away from the building. There were about ten kids there: me and my brother; the Matz brothers- Louis, Stuey, and Dooey; the Motley brothers- Todd, Doug, and Scott, the Hanson boys and Kathy Baker. I wanted to invite Man, but there wasn't time. My brother had us rushing over. And I remembered what Man had told me about not seeing him anymore. I wondered if he meant it.

Greg was working on the trash can for a few minutes. He stood up and said, "All right, boys and girls, are you ready?" Everyone shouted, "Yeah!" Greg pointed to the trash can and said, "So after this thing blows, we all go through that hole in the fence that goes to the park and then walk, don't run home. I am not going to tell you where I got the nitro, but I got it, and then I created the fuse and igniter. This is the first time I've done this; I am not quite sure it is going to work. In other words, stand back!" Everybody moved back, about twenty feet from the trash can. Two Matz brothers Louis and Stuey were at opposite ends behind the store's loading area to make sure the coast was clear and that nobody was coming. They gave the thumbs up and came running back to where we all were standing. Greg lit the fuse and ran to us. We waited. Nothing. "Something must have gone wrong," Greg said. And then BOOM! The trash can exploded; the metal sides blowing out like banana leaves. It was extremely loud. There was a cloud of smoke, and as it dissipated Greg yelled, "Let's go!"

We all hurriedly climbed through a hole in the wall that led to the park. The Motley brothers started running home. "Stupid idiots," Greg spat. I had seen a great many things that Greg had devised, but the way he got that trash can to blow up was impressive. And beautiful.

CHAPTER 39

I wanted to tell Man about Greg blowing up the trash can. Figured he could use a distraction. I knocked on his front door. It was Monday at around 10 a.m. Monday. I thought his dad would be at work. He usually worked during the week and had weekends off. Their doorbell had the exact same ring as my house, something called the Friedland Westminster Chime, two sequences of four musical notes played in rotation. Your classic suburban melody. Mr. Pacheco answered the door.

"Is Man home?"

"Yes, but he can't come to the door right now."

"Oh."

"Gerald, I wanted to show you something."

Mr. Pacheco opened the screen door, and he stepped out. He grabbed me by the arm, firmly but not too harshly. He led me to the flowerbed in front of the house. There was a crucifix on its side and a hole in the ground. "Do you know what that is, Gerald?"

I shook my head.

"That's a grave. And do you know what I found there?"

Again, I shook my head. He reached into the pocket of his gray guayabera and pulled out a dead sparrow and a small picture frame with a photo of a woman.

"Do you know who that is?"

I shook my head reflexively, but I knew who it was.

"That's Manuel's mom. He made his own grave for her even though she has one at Forest Lawn. I don't know what is wrong with that boy. But he can't play today."

Frightened by his clenched tone I nodded my head and said, "Okay."

"Let me ask you a question, Gerald. You love your mother, don't you?" I nodded my head.

"Of course you do. All boys love their mother. Almost all boys. And you would never want anything bad to happen to her, like what happened to Manuel's mom. You heard about that, didn't you? Man told you."

"He told me that she died."

"That's all he said about it?"

Again I nodded my head.

"Okay, you better go home now." He turned and went into the house.

CHAPTER 40

Kathy and I were at the enclave, sitting on milk crates and looking out onto the expanse of dirt. "My father had to be taken to the hospital last night. He choked on a piece of meat. My mom couldn't get it out. He coughed and coughed. Finally, it came out, but he had a heart attack or something. Anyway, he's at the hospital." I touched her hand. She squeezed my hand and said "He's going to be okay. That's what my mom said the doctor said. Still, it was weird. His face was all red and his eyes were puffing out. He looked so helpless."

We sat quietly for a little while. Then we looked at each other. We kissed. And the way we kissed was just touching lips, nothing more than that—just touching lips, but not exactly. Like how they kissed in the movies. I could remember when I was very young, before I went to school, and my brother was at school and my father at work, the movies that my mother and I used to watch. And in those movies, how they kissed. I tried to emulate that. Which meant my lips were not exactly on her lips, a little to the side. I learned later it was called a stage kiss. For a long time, every time I kissed a girl, it was a stage kiss. But Kathy didn't seem to mind.

"I better get home; my dad is coming back from the hospital today." We walked back to our block. It was a hot and sunny day, but there was a little breeze. It felt like summer was coming to an end. We stopped in her driveway. I said, "School will be starting soon." She shook her head and said, "I am not looking forward to that." Neither was I. The only good thing was I could hang out with Miss Murakami in the library and listen to records.

I watched Kathy go into her house. She stopped; sensing I was watching her. I waved and smiled at her. I started walking back to my house, I thought of going to see Man. I wanted to stop and check in on him, but I was hungry, so I figured I would go home and have a sandwich and a glass of milk and then try him. When I got home my mom's car, a yellow Plymouth Valiant that my grandparents had given us, was parked in the driveway with the trunk open. I saw the back of Mr. Pacheco entering my house; he was carrying a couple bags of groceries. Mom came out and smiled as she passed him. She went to the trunk and grabbed the other bags of groceries, closed the trunk with her elbow, and went into the house.

After she was in the house, I walked to the side of the house where there was a window, and from that window I looked into the kitchen. There was Mom and Mr. Pacheco putting the bags of groceries down on the counter. I heard her thank him; she seemed a little uncomfortable, a little rigid. Mr. Pacheco was smiling. He had on yellow shorts, white tank top and flip-flops. His legs were hairy, and the shirt had no sleeves so you could see his big muscles. They stood quietly for a minute and then the phone rang. My mom looked relieved. Mr. Pacheco said goodbye and left the house.

After I saw him leave, I went into the house. Mom was still on the phone. "How long has he been gone?" And I watched her as she listened to what the person was saying at the other end of the line. "Okay, if you hear anything, let me know. As soon as possible." She hung up the phone, turned, put her hands to her face and rubbed her eyes.

I went inside the house. She lifted her head, and then she saw me. She smiled. As if seeing me made her troubles go away. But only for a second. "Hi, GG."

CHAPTER 41

I was in the living room doing my homework on the sofa. My parents were in the kitchen talking. I heard my mom tell my dad, "Uncle Dan has gone missing. Maria says he has been gone for two weeks. His episodes were getting worse. Maria told him he had to leave again. She couldn't take it anymore. He was acting crazy. He said he was going to stay at Danny Junior's apartment. But he never showed up. She doesn't want to call the police. Not just yet."

My father said, "Why don't you ask Erik Estrada next door, see if he could help?"

"I don't know. There's something about that guy."

"What do you mean? You never say anything bad about anyone."

"That's not true."

"Yeah, well, he's a joke. I don't go for all that machismo business."

"Yeah, well, maybe that's why I love you."

"What are you saying? That I'm not macho?"

"Un poquito."

I peeked around the corner and saw Mom put her arms around my dad. They kissed lightly.

Dad said, "Well, maybe I should go and talk to Mr. Chips. I mean, if you don't want to call the cops but also maybe need the cops, there's got to be an upside to having a cop living on the block."

"No, I'll give him a call. After all, Man and Gerald are pretty good friends. I should reach out to Mrs. Pacheco, too."

"Yes, where is this Mrs. Pacheco?"

Dad went in to watch the baseball game with Kenny. I went into the kitchen and made myself a glass of Ovaltine. I saw my mom pull out a piece of paper from the pocket of one of the homemade dresses, royal blue with a tapered faux fur around the pockets, collar, and hem. The dress seemed almost too fancy to be handmade. And the color of the dress seemed to vibrate. She sat down at the counter, read the number from the paper, and spun the rotary dial on the banana yellow wall phone. "Hello? Hello, Mrs. Pacheco."

CHAPTER 42

Have you ever noticed that G.I. Joes don't have a pecker?" I asked Man. He laughed and I pulled down the pants of a Joe dressed as an infantry man. "Look, nothing there. All smooth." Man laughed again. It was good to see him laugh. A regular laugh. Not that hissing thing that he was doing. He leaned over to pick up a Joe dressed like a cop. From around his neck a crucifix dangled out of his shirt. There it was, Jesus nailed to the cross. "Do you always wear that?"

"I told you."

"Even when you go swimming?"

"I don't go swimming. I don't know how."

"Oh yeah. If I had a real swimming pool, I would swim every day."

"I don't know how to swim," Man said again bitterly.

"Why don't you learn?" I said growing frustrated at Man's resignation.

"Because I don't want to!"

Not wanting to let the subject of the crucifix go I asked him tauntingly, "Isn't it weird to have that around your neck? You know, a man nailed to a cross, around your neck. All the time."

"Jesus died for our sins, it's the least I could do," he said sarcastically.

"What does it mean, died for our sins?"

"I don't know exactly. Like, because he died, nobody has to go to hell, no matter how many bad things you do."

"So, since Jesus is there, there is nobody in hell."

"Heaven is only for the people who believe in him. Hell is for people who don't."

"So, if you don't believe in him, you go to hell, even if you don't do bad things. But the people who do bad things, even really bad things, will go to heaven as long as they wear a cross around their neck?"

"Something like that."

"Do you believe that?"

"No. That's just what my stupid dad says."

"Doesn't make any sense."

"Yeah. I know."

We didn't say anything for a while. I could hear Mom and Mrs. Pacheco talking in the kitchen and I could hear a baseball game upstairs. I was getting bored and kind of wished I was watching the Angels too. Seemed like I hadn't watched or been to a game in a long time. No matter that they were really bad and hardly ever won a game; they were my team. I liked the players. They were nice to me. When I went to the games, we would get there early for batting practice and then when they were done the players would come over and sign autographs. Sometimes they'd give me a baseball. A real live major league baseball ball. Since the team wasn't very good, not too many people cared if they got Rudy Meoli's autograph. But I did. And the players appreciated the attention. Who knows how much longer before they'd be sent down to the minors? I just wished that Man liked baseball or the Beatles so we could have other things to talk about besides his father.

"Well, I better go and make dinner," I heard my mom tell Mrs. Pacheco. "Me too." Mrs. Pacheco replied. They walked out of the dining room and into the living room. They looked down at us quietly playing. "They're such nice boys," Mrs. Pacheco said.

Mom closed her arms around herself in an embrace and said, "Mine can be a little rascal sometimes."

"Mine too," Mrs. Pacheco said, only when she said it things became uncomfortable because Man was not hers. And everybody knew it.

Mr. Pacheco came down the stairs and into the living room. "You missed a good game, boys. The Angels finally won." He put his arm around Mrs. Pacheco and pulled her close to him "Hello, Rachel," he said to my mom. "Nice of you to come and visit."

"I have heard so much about Man, Manuel from Gerald. He is so glad you guys moved to our block. And what a nice home you have."

"I'm glad we did too." Mr. Pacheco said, sounding vaguely insincere. They were acting. I could always tell when grownups were acting. It was so obvious. Their voices changed, losing all musicality, and their movements stiff and calculated.

"Have you been having a nice summer?" Mom asked Mr. Pacheco.

"Oh yes, very nice. I have been taking it easy. Decided to take a week off. Take some of my vacation time, instead of taking a trip, just take it easy. Lying around the house, watching baseball games, and being with my family."

"Yes, it's so important to do that." Mom said. Her acting was better than his, but she was still acting. Until she said, "I was sorry to hear about Man's friend. How terrible."

Man, and I gave the appearance of being engrossed with playing with the Joes, as if we weren't listening. But we were listening.

"Yes, terrible. And to make it worse, a detective I worked with was the driver."

"He was having a lot of problems," Mrs. Pacheco interjected.

"Oh yeah?" Mom replied.

"It's stressful, you know, being a detective, some turn to booze."

"What's going to happen to him?"

"He had already been suspended from the force. And now he must face felony hit-and-run and possibly manslaughter charges. Doesn't look good for him."

"That's just so sad."

"What can you do? The job is stressful and some have trouble coping."

"There was something I wanted to ask you about, in a sort of unofficial way. If that's okay. My big brother seems to have gone missing."

"Oh, yes?"

"It's been two weeks. His wife had asked him to move out of the house and he was supposed to move in with his oldest son, but he never showed up. You see, he is what they call manic depressive, and he drinks."

"I see. Well, if I can be of any service. Did you file a report?"

"No. His wife would rather not. She doesn't want him to get into any trouble, but she is very worried."

"I understand. Maybe I can help. In an unofficial capacity. At least at first. Why don't you write down some information, his name and address, and I will see what I can do."

"Really?"

"Of course."

"That would be great. I can't thank enough."

"Least we can do," Mrs. Pacheco said. "We are so grateful for your son's friendship with Manny. He's such a loner."

CHAPTER 43

Do you think Uncle Dan is alright?" I said to Mom as we were walking home from Man's house. "I don't know, GG. I don't know."

"Mom?"

"Yeah?"

"I don't like Mr. Pacheco."

"Why do you say that?"

"Some things Man has told me."

"Do you want to tell me?"

"I told Man that I wouldn't tell anyone."

"I'm not just anyone. I'm your mom."

I thought about telling her what Man had told me, about seeing his dad kill his mom. As I tried to put it into words and imagined what the words would sound like coming out of my mouth. It didn't seem real. And I didn't want to make my mom feel bad or scared. And I remembered Man had told me to not talk about it to anyone, and what Mr. Pacheco had told me too, the way he asked me if I loved my mom. And I felt he would do something bad to us if he found out. And anyway, it didn't matter if someone accused him of it, or if Man told people what he saw. Nobody would believe him. Or me for that matter.

"Sometimes he yells at Man."

"Oh. Is that all?" she said indulgently.

"Mom?"

"Yeah?"

"Do you believe in Jesus Christ?"

"Why do you ask that?"

"Because Man wears that cross around his neck, and we were talking about it."

"I was brought up going to church. Papa Joe is very religious, you know."

"I know. He has a big cross around his neck too."

"I think Jesus was a very good man, I just don't know about the rest of it. But I'm not like your dad."

"He's an atheist."

"Yes. It's no big secret. You can make up your own mind. I think church is a good thing. It is a good way to have a community. And I believe in prayer. Papa Joe prays every night. It helps him. I think- it is like talking to yourself in some ways. It's a good way to give yourself comfort."

We walked down our street. The sun's orange had faded behind the Cypress trees and the rooftops of the suburban homes. We sat down on the front lawn of my house. About four inches thick of dark green grass. The grass tickled my naked legs. It had been only recently that my father started allowing my brother to push the gas-powered lawn mower. I was jealous and pestered my father to allow me to push the machine, but he said that I wasn't old enough. He didn't know that my brother let me do it when my father was not around. I didn't realize until I started reading the Mark Twain novels, that my brother was pulling a Tom Sawyer move in allowing me to push the lawnmower. He hated mowing the lawn.

Mom held my hand, and I felt comfortable, and I thought that she, not Man, was my real best friend. Who was Man anyway? I had only known him for a few weeks and already all this death and weird stuff had happened. And this threat, this not-so-veiled threat to my mom by this monster of a man. And I wished that they had never moved to our block.

Now Uncle Dan was missing. He was the only adult who talked to me and us kids like he was a kid, or like we were adults, or more like we were just people. No separate language. Funny, silly, sincere, observant, looking at the world with truth, a kind of truth that was different from any other grown-up, even Mom. I remember once Uncle Dan once told me, "Some people say there is going to be another war, and all the shows on TV are warning us or showing us how there is going to be another war, and how this war will be the very last war and will wipe out the whole human race, and how somehow we deserved to be wiped out because of what we did to the planet or because we no longer believe in God, but none of that is going to happen. Nobody believes in God anyway. Especially the people who say they believe in God; they are the ones who don't believe in God the most. The question is not; do you believe in God; it is does God believe in us? Either way, the human race is not going anywhere anytime soon."

What the hell happened to my Uncle Dan?

On the day of my birthday party, after Man had destroyed the piñata, I saw Uncle Dan talking to Man. What were they talking about? They were at the other end of the yard. Mostly Man talking, but Uncle Dan listening intently. And then I saw how Mr. Pacheco was watching them. Watching them with a blank look on his face.

Mom said to me, "Don't worry, everything will be alright. Uncle Dan will show up, and when he does, we better make sure he gets the help he needs. I don't think he has ever gotten over the death of his son. He himself saw some terrible things in the Korean War. He was in the infantry. He wasn't as lucky as your dad. Before going he had plans to be a priest but when he came back, he had changed his mind, to Papa Joe's great disappointment. He is a very sensitive person. Sometimes the world can get to be too much for someone like that. Someone who feels things so deeply. So, that means, you must always be willing to ask for help."

She took me in her arms. I felt her warm body against mine. I could smell her perfume, smelled like roses. She ran her hand over my cheek. I took her hand and held it. She gave mine a little squeeze. She started to hum the song by the Beatles, Hey Jude. Very quietly. Her chest vibrated as she hummed. I put my head deeper against her bosom and she held me ever tighter. Now, I could hear both her heartbeat and the humming.

CHAPTER 44

I got on my skateboard and made my left leg propel it to Greg Gibson's house. I wasn't a great skater. I couldn't do any tricks aside from a 360. I mostly used it as transportation. Every kid had one, it was integral to being a kid in Southern California. Some kids my age had already started surfing. I was not interested. Seemed like too much work and expense. Where was I going to get the money for a surfboard and a wetsuit anyway? Who was going to take me to the beach at the crack of dawn, which is when the waves were best. I didn't feel or look like the surfer kids, with their blonde hair and laconic demeanor.

I knocked on Greg's front door which was at the other end of the block. A house just like ours but with a reversed floor plan. Same yard and hedge separating it from the adjoining property. His mom answered the door. A nice woman with a kind face. Kind, but tired and sad. Greg's dad had left her a few months prior. Or she kicked him out. The story kept changing. She welcomed me cheerily enough. "He's in his lab in the garage." She pointed me to the door off the living room.

Greg sat at a makeshift desk, with goggles on, mixing something with two vials. He looked over to see me. "Gerald! Howdy doody. Come here and take a look at this." He poured the two vials into a large beaker; it began to smoke, and a purple cloud ascended from it. And the aroma of watermelon filled the air. "It worked!" We looked at each other and laughed. Not only was it beautiful, but it smelled really good.

"That trash can. The way you exploded that trash can was

really cool."

"Yeah, it turned out better than I thought it was going to. In fact, I wasn't quite sure if it was going to work at all. The thing with nitro is you have to have the proper fuse to ignite it. Some people think that all you gotta do is shake it and it explodes, but that's not how it works."

"So cool. Where'd you get it?"

"What?"

"The nitro."

"Ha ha. Well, if I tell you, will you promise not to tell anyone?"

"Yes. Definitely."

"I broke into a welding shop."

"You stole it?"

"Property is theft."

"What?"

"Never mind. So, what's going on?"

I sat down on another stool. "Do you know the new kid, Manuel?" I asked him.

"I've seen him around. Is he cool?"

"Yeah. He's cool. Only…"

"Only what?"

"Well, his dad is weird."

"Whose dad is not. My dad left, you know."

"Yeah. I know."

"He was having an affair, I guess. My mom found out and kicked him out."

"I'm sorry about that."

"I heard them arguing, you know, and he apologized and everything. But she wouldn't—well, she told him to leave. The thing is, I haven't seen him since. My dad is cool. He gave me all this stuff." He looked at the stool I was sitting on. "He's a scientist, you know."

"Yeah. I know. You told me."

"That's just how things go. Look at insects; they are driven by their sex drive. Everything they do is driven by that. It drives them insane. Take bees, for instance. The male, after he has sex with the queen bee, his dick pops off and he dies. Humans are no different."

"That is so weird!"

"It's true. The female praying mantis eats the male during sex. Humans can be evil but they're not alone. What about Manuel's dad?"

"I don't know. He's kind of scary."

"Well, he's a cop. But I know. I've seen him out there, always mowing his lawn, with those mirrored sunglasses. Definitely menacing-looking. Did he do something to you?"

"No, but Man told me a few things."

"Like what?"

I was thinking if I should tell Greg. The smartest kid on the block by a mile, and always nice to me. He had wisdom beyond his years. He was thirteen years old but had skipped two grades and was already starting high school in the fall. The way he spoke it seemed like he understood everything.

"If he asked you not to tell anyone, that's okay, you don't have to tell me. But if something happens and you get scared, you can tell me. I will help you."

I thanked him and went back home.

I passed by the Pacheco's on my skateboard. Mr. Pacheco was pruning his rose bushes with small handheld shears. He had on a Hawaiian shirt, those mirrored sunglasses and a blank expression. I hit a crack on the sidewalk and went flying off my skateboard. I was an expert at tucking and rolling, but still I skinned my knee badly. Same knee that I had skinned in Arizona. The scab peeled off. I sat up, pulled my knee up, and examined the scrape. The skin was filled with dirt and little rocks. It stung terribly.

"Are you alright?" I looked up and there he was.

"I am all right," I said with a few tears rolling down my face. I cried every time I got hurt, automatically, no matter how severe the injury; and they were mostly not too severe.

This injury was about the size of a silver dollar. He took off his sunglasses and examined my wound.

"Come with me and let's get that cleaned off."

I walked with him to the patio, carrying my skateboard and limping as I went. He sat me down on the patio chair, one of those florid yellow table-and-chair sets with the matching umbrella, near the flowerbed where the grave of the bird had been. Now, there was nothing, just a small hole in the ground. He went into the garage and came out with a first aid kit in his hand.

With a garden hose, water very gently trickling out, he washed the scrape. He put some Neosporin on it, then he took some gauze and wiped the wound and then placed a large bandage over the scrape.

"Are you okay? Does it hurt very much?"

With tears still trickling from my eyes, I said, "No."

He smiled and said okay. The way he smiled; it was like he was a completely different person from the image that I had formed of him in my mind. He was gentle and paternal. In that instant it again seemed unfathomable that he was capable of doing the things that Man had said he had done.

When I got home Mom asked me what happened to my knee. "I fell riding my skateboard. Hit a crack in the sidewalk."

"Who put on the bandage?"

I hesitated. I knew that Mr. Pacheco's kindness to me that day didn't align with how I had described him to my mom. But I had to tell her the truth. "Man's dad did."

"See, he's not so bad."

I knew she was going to say that. She was always trying to look for the good in people. Even Richard Nixon. At the same time, she was aware when someone's bad intentions outweighed any possibility of reformation. Like Richard Nixon. She wasn't naive, she was a humanist. Her philosophy in life emphasized both empathy and naturalism. Humans are driven by something almost inexplicable and that we all make mistakes, we are all on a path of learning how to function best for ourselves and for and in society. But at a certain point, one runs out of chances. And then one is not only irredeemable but also a nuisance, sometimes a deadly nuisance.

CHAPTER 45

On my father's dresser was a beautiful wooden box, walnut and on the lid a pearl inlay in the shape of a diamond. Every now and then I'd pull over a chair and snatch a nickel or a dime from his change cup and go buy a candy bar at the store, taking a brief gander at his beautiful humidor. One day I pulled the chair over and opened the box. It was filled with cigars. He smoked cigars when he was doing yardwork or cooking or driving in the car. I loved the smell of his cigars. They smelled dark and dense. Cigars were an integral part of who he was. I often thought about how the things we do, the way we dress, the way we smell, what we think about, even dream about, these are the things that make us who we are. And if there is a god, I was open to the possibility; he, she, it or they assigned these things to us, individually. I reached in and grabbed a cigar. Put it under my shirt and in the belt of my pants. I went into the kitchen, in the utility drawer there was a matchbook. I took that.

I opened the garage door just wide enough to crawl under. I let close the big door, the giant springs on either side prevented it from slamming. I went to the back of the garage, sat down in the dark, on the cold concrete, took the cigar out of its plastic wrapper, and stuck the wrapper in my pants pocket. I pulled the matchbook from my pocket and after three attempts got a match to strike and ignite. I put the cigar in my mouth and put the flame to it. I sucked and sucked but nothing happened. Then I remembered seeing my father bite off the end before lighting it. I put down the matchbook, put the cigar end between my teeth and took a little bite and spat out a little chunk. I picked up the matchbook and on the first strike got one lit. I put the flame to the end of the cigar and lit the thing, puffing like I had seen my father do. I took one great pull and quickly exhaled. A blue gray cloud of smoke, which I could only make out by the burning ember from the tip of the cigar. It tasted nice, spicey. It tasted like my dad, like in some way I was smoking the essence of my father. The tip of the cigar was now glowing orange. It looked like Halloween.

The garage door sprung open. Light flooded in. I heard my brother's voice; he was with his friend Doug. "I smell something." They walked to the back of the garage; I snuffed out the cigar on the concrete floor, but it was too late. He saw me and said, "You've been smoking one of Dad's cigars!" I denied it, but it was no use. He had me. "I am going to TELL!" I pleaded with him. "For your own good. A) you are a thief, and B) you are way too young to be smoking a cigar." I implored him not to tell my father, who when he lost his temper, was like a volcano erupting. "Okay, but you have to be my slave." I asked him what he meant by being his slave. "In other words, you have to do anything I say."

"No way!"

"Fine. I will tell Dad." I agreed to be his slave.

For the rest of the day, I was his servant. I got him his drink when he asked, changed the channel when he wanted; and we had to watch whatever show he wanted.

That night after dinner there was the Marx Brothers movie Duck Soup on television. I was looking forward to it, but Kenny said, even though it had been agreed upon that I could have this one wish granted, he had changed his mind and that we were going to watch a World War 2 documentary. I told him he could rat on me if he wanted, but I was watching Duck Soup. Since nobody wants to be a snitch, and since there might be something that I could snitch on him for in the future, it was in his interest to not press the point.

I watched the movie by myself. I hadn't seen this one before and ironically it was a war movie. Even the Marx Brothers were going to war. But their war was literally a joke. And when they sang, *"They got guns, we got guns, all god's children got guns!"* Playing banjos, jumping up and down and all over Margret Dumont, I was laughing so hard I thought I'd pee my pants. Groucho smoked his big cigar and made snide and funny quips. I put one and one together, my father was Groucho, and I was my dad therefore I was Groucho. Only I really felt like Harpo. And Harpo, without saying a word, was the funniest of them all. I envied his overcoat, everything was in his overcoat- enormously long scissors, blow torches, a hot cup of coffee, even a record player. When he felt pain he cried, open mouth and silent, overwrought, and when he thought something funny he laughed uproariously. All without sound. Without words. Words are unnecessary. Words are redundant. Everything said, can be said with one's eyes and mouth and body, more honestly than words. Words are lies. One word has too many meanings so that there is no meaning, which is why words are easily manipulated. Words are the world of adults. Once words are introduced to a child that is when the confusion begins. And the lies and lying. Never to be remedied. Never.

But words are beautiful too. All the words in the books that I read. The books of C.S. Lewis and Frank Baum and Antoine de Saint-Expery and Lewis Carroll and Charles Dickens. And I wrote stories made from words. And it felt good when the right word, placed correctly, made a sentence sing. And the songs of the Beatles and the words in their lyrics reached me and gave me comfort. Their words were poetry. And Man wrote poetry. I wanted to see Man's poetry. I had never read poetry. I wanted to read Man's poetry.

It wasn't too late after the Marx Brothers movie ended. I walked over to Man's house. On the way there I stopped at the tree in front of our house. There was a bird there making a song. If the bird had been there before and had sung this song, this same song, I hadn't noticed. Its song was almost metallic. The sound of it. Clipped chirps followed by an ascending then descending melody which sped up and slowed down. And it was loud and repeated over and over. I looked up into the branches of the tree. The bird sat there, motionless, singing stoically. Nothing strange or exotic about the bird. Just a plain brown bird. It looked like a Sparrow, only larger. And its song was strong and the way it perched, so still, dignified, impressed me. All alone up in that tree. And the sound was relentless, it filled my ears and my head.

I didn't have to go to Man's house because he was right in front of me. "I could hear this bird all the way from my house," he said.

"Yeah, it's loud. I wonder what it's singing about."

"He is calling. Calling for a ladybird."

"Oh, you mean. A mate."

"Yes, a mate."

"So, he sings his song and a ladybird hears the song and says to herself, I like that song, I want to meet the singer of that song. And she flies over and lands on the branch next to him and then they fall in love, just like that."

"I don't know about the falling in love part. But they mate. And then they, or she, lays some eggs and the cycle of life continues."

"So, if we just stayed here, we could watch that happen."

"If we had all night."

We looked up in the tree and watched him singing his song.

"He looks kind of tired," I said.

"His old mate might have died. That's why he is out here singing his song at the end of summer."

"Oh." I looked at Man looking up at the bird. It still amazed me how pretty he was, for a boy. And his very long dark brown eyelashes. "I wanted to ask you something."

He looked away from the bird and at me. "Yeah?"

"I want to read your poetry. I've never read poetry before."

"Oh. You can't."

"Why not?" I said, a little irritated.

"Because I burned all of my poetry, and I am never going to write again."

"You did?"

"But I remember one by heart. I will tell it to you.

The Aztec boys angle over the balcony
chewing gum made of resin
from the sapodilla tree;
it was the dead of night
the moon was pregnant

they heard the first shot
and then the next
and then
one by one
they jumped

CHAPTER 46

Mickey and Pluto jogging around the circumference of the bowl. The bowl had been kept in the bottom drawer of the kitchen cabinet along with a few of the items that I used to play with while Mom was working in the kitchen. It had been a while since I played with those things let alone ate from that bowl. I was watching Captain Kangaroo on the little portable television sitting on the counter opposite me and eating fruit loops out of my Disney "mousercise" bowl.

Even though I was perhaps a bit too old for the show I still enjoyed it. It made me feel more like the kid that I was before Man moved to our block.

The phone rang. The ringing disturbed my meditation on bygone things. It rang a few times. Nobody picked up. I did not want to answer it. I did not want to hear who might be on the other end. And so, I let it keep ringing. Finally, my mother came into the kitchen, "GG, answer the phone!" As she was coming over to pick it up for herself, I did not want her to hear what might be Dad's girlfriend on the other end, so I abruptly picked it up. I held it to my ear, but I did not say anything. "Hello." It was a man's voice. Gruff, stern, "Hello," annoyed. My mother took the receiver from me. "Hello....Oh hi...You're kidding! Is he okay?... Oh, thank you so much.... we'll be right over."

In the car, on the radio, the song- *Do You Know the Way to San Jose?* played. Mom was singing along. Sitting beside her in the front seat of the car, looking out the window at the houses and the trees, I asked her, "Where are we going?"

"To get Uncle Dan."

"Where is he?"

"At the police station."

She pulled her car into the station parking lot. We got out and walked past the shiny black and white Chevy Malibu's, the sun refracting almost blindingly off the chrome bumpers. We entered an enormously cool lobby with wooden benches against the wall where sat a few handcuffed men. The expression on each face was one of utter defeat.

At the front desk Mom asked for Officer Pacheco. A short time later he came out, in plain clothes, walking side by side with Uncle Dan, who seemed tired, and scruffy with a scraggly beard. Yet he was cheered to see us. Mr. Pacheco gestured towards Uncle Dan amiably and said, "We found him sleeping in his car near the Seal Beach pier. At first, he didn't want to come but I explained that I was your friend." Uncle Dan smiled ironically. "I went with him because I didn't feel I had a choice. But that's okay. Where's my car?"

Uncle Dan couldn't go back home to Maria, she wouldn't have him. She loved him. There was no question of that. He was all she knew of love. All she ever wanted to know. And after him she knew she couldn't love again. She had been depleted of so much. But at least she had those initial years where it would be impossible to find two people more swept up in the idea of romance, of kismet, of fate.

They had met after Uncle Dan had got back from the war. He was doing well in the insurance racket; in fact he was at the top of his game. They met at a church social in Long Beach. She had been born and raised in Long Beach. Her father owned a very successful chain of supermarkets which he ended up selling to a larger chain. That move proved to be a big mistake. But when Uncle Dan and Maria met, not only they, but the whole country was experiencing a boom. She was young, college educated, emancipated woman of twenty-two years of age. He was opinionated, wrote poetry and unlike any other man she had ever met was emotionally open. And they were beautiful. They looked like a Mexican version of Myrna Loy and William Powell. There was barely any indication that Uncle Dan was less than well- mentally, spiritually.

They had four children in succession. The fifth was lost in childbirth. That was when Uncle Dan had his first episode. He stayed drunk for two weeks. Maria placed him in a sanitorium to dry out. His grief displaced her own, so busy was she taking care of him and making excuses to his job and other commitments, all the while looking after the four boys. When he got out of the sanatorium he went back to work, and things seemed fine. They had one more child, Darlene. But when their eldest son Darrell was killed in Vietnam, Uncle Dan lost it, and he never got it back.

He knew that he couldn't go on living out of his car because it would cause too much worry for his family. Plus, he was sure to get picked up again. Mom insisted that he live with us. When we got home, she told him to take a shower while she prepared a meal. When he came out, he looked better. He had shaved, except for his mustache, and combed his black hair back. "I borrowed Robinson's razor. I'll buy him new razor blades." Mom told him not to be ridiculous. We sat down in the living room, drank coca colas from the bottle and had a late lunch.

My father came home. He saw Uncle Dan and smiled, genuinely glad to see he was alright. Mom explained that Uncle Dan would be staying with us for a little while. Dad smiled and said, "Sure, of course." But Uncle Dan could sense his reluctance and so insisted he would live out of a pup tent in our backyard until he got some money together to get his own place. He said he didn't mind. He would pitch it every night and take it down every morning; and he wouldn't be a bother. It was a strange arrangement but then again Uncle Dan was a little strange.

Mom helped Uncle Dan put up fliers around at the super-markets and stores advertising his work as a handyman. Mom liked having him around. Her older brother. A truly thought-ful man. A man who felt things so deeply they cut him and left little scars on his consciousness. She said he reminded her of Papa Joe, when Papa Joe was a young man, even though Uncle Dan wasn't young anymore he retained a youthfulness. But he was troubled. Something not right in his physiology. He said he was a Spiritual Alchemist, everything he did was an attempt to break down memories and traumas and put them right, to free his spiritual self, which was trapped and trying to transcend worldly pain. Life work. But nothing to cry about.

I liked having him there. Especially as my dad wasn't around as much. He was having more business meetings in the evening.

CHAPTER 47

We were at the park sitting on the grass. The sun directly overhead was emitting the kind of heat and infrared light that made one feel like they were on Mars but was normal for this part of summer. "This is the last time that you will see me," Man said, as if he was telling me the weather forecast. I laughed. Though I knew he was not joking, or at least not trying to be funny. I looked at the kids playing basketball and then I looked at him, at the side of his head, his profile, black hair long in back, front bangs resting on his forehead, the long eyelashes, a small bump of a nose and dark pink lips slightly open. I touched his arm. He pulled it away. I touched it again and he pulled it away again. He was making me angry. I wanted to touch him, to bring him back to a physical reality. He was living too much in his head. I grabbed his arm again. He pulled it away and with his other hand, with his fist, he hit me in the face. I screamed, "You jerk!" And shoved him.

We rolled around on the ground and then I got on top of him, straddled him and held his hands down with my hands. It was no contest. I was much stronger than him. My face was directly over his. I stared down at him. And then I puckered my lips and let drip out a little stream of saliva. Just as it was about to break off and go splattering on his face, I sucked it back. I did this a few times. I was expecting him to get mad or disgusted, but nothing. No reaction. So, I got off him.

"The thing is," he said, breathing hard. "I am just like him."

"No, you're not. That's stupid. You're nothing like him."

"Oh Gerald. Your head is in the clouds. I think if things were different. I think I could show you many things. Help you understand how things really are."

"What are you talking about?"

"I said I am just like my dad and I am. I could kill. I know that I could. It's in my blood. I have killed. I have killed things. I could kill him. That is where we are different Gerald. I don't think you are like that. You don't have that in your blood. Or maybe you do, but it's more buried."

"What have you killed?" I asked him.

"You don't want to know. You have this whole idea about, you know, good and evil. And if you don't do evil then you are innocent. Like an angel. But who is to say what is evil?"

"Killing is evil. It's what evil is. More than anything."

"I suppose. But it doesn't really matter. Nothing matters."

A few butterflies fluttered by and landed on the marigolds at our feet. We both noticed them. "Do you want to kill those butterflies," I asked him. He laughed. "Why would I do that? They're really beautiful." His answer made me feel better. "Besides. What good would it do?"

He got up, picked up his bike and got on it, one leg on the ground holding him up. He looked away and then he looked at me. "Remember what I told you. Don't talk to anyone about what you know about my family. Just pretend you never met me. I know you probably wish you hadn't." He rode away. I stayed watching the butterflies. After a while I got up and went over and joined the basketball game.

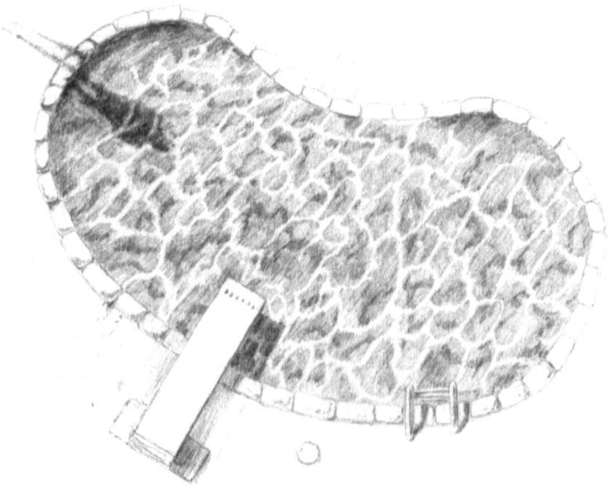

CHAPTER 48

Sitting on my perch in the rubber tree, looking through my binoculars at Man's backyard I spotted Man and his dad standing by the swimming pool. Mr. Pacheco was pointing his finger at Man, jabbing his finger into his chest, slowly and repeatedly. He loomed over him. Wearing swim trunks, no shirt and those mirrored sunglasses. Man stared up at him; his face, as usual, showed no emotion. He stared at his dad, his eyes winnowed, maybe it was anger, or a certain kind of fearlessness. He wasn't flinching. He opened his mouth to scream, and he screamed, but no sound came from his mouth.

Finally, Mr. Pacheco raised his fist. Man stared up at him, smiled and pointed at his face and then grabbed his dick in a grand and fearless display of machismo. Mr. Pacheco shook his head. He got down on one knee, grabbed Man by the shoulders, leaned into his ear and said something to him. Man's countenance got serious. They pulled apart though still locked into each other's eyes. Man smiled, half-smile. Mr. Pacheco slapped Man across the face. Man, with wide eyes and puckered lips spat on the ground in front of Mr. Pacheco, who looked down at the spit, shook his head again, got to his feet and walked into the house.

Man rubbed his face which now had a red mark on it. From his eyes water came. He wiped them with the back of his hand. He walked over to the pool and looked in. He looked around, and then up at the sky. He stared straight away. He jumped into the pool and then started slowly sinking. His body descending as if all of life had gone from it, arms akimbo, an inanimate object. I watched him through the binoculars, watched his motionless body sinking. I thought that I would climb down from the tree and go into my house and get help for Man. But I couldn't move.

Then he moved, in a spasm, and then another. He struggled and wiggled. Like a guppy. He made his way to the surface of the water and then to the side of the pool using jerky movements to propel himself. He put his hand on the edge of the pool and pulled his head out of the water. He held on to the side of the pool, breathing heavy, trying to catch his breath. It looked like he was about to get out.

Mr. Pacheco walked up to Man, got down on his knees, and put his hand on the top of Man's head and his other hand on Man's shoulder. He pushed Man underwater and held him there. That is when I climbed down from the tree.

I ran into the kitchen and found my mother who was preparing lunch. "Mom! I was in the tree out back, and, and, and, I saw Man jump into the pool, and, and, he doesn't know how to swim, and he sank but then he got to the side of the pool, but his father pushed him under." She got down to my level and looked me in the eyes. "Are you sure GG?" I nodded my head. "Okay." She picked up the wall phone and dialed. "Nobody answering at the Pacheco's. Now, are you sure that's what you saw?" Again, I nodded my head. She picked up the phone again and dialed zero.

We ran over to Man's house, but nobody answered the

doorbell. We walked around to the side of the house to the backyard. There was Man on the ground with Mr. Pacheco, dripping water, giving him mouth-to-mouth resuscitation. He pulled back, put his ear to Man's chest. Then sat back on the ground with his knees up, he put his hands on his face and began to weep. He didn't seem to know that we were there.

There was Man's lifeless body. His eyes open, staring up at the sky. Who was this kid? Was any of this real? I had known him, this kid, and played with him and talked to him and he had told me so many things that changed who I was and how I saw the world and now he was dead? What does that mean? I'll never see him again? Impossible! You mean he is no longer a person, just a thing? Like a sack of potatoes. What happens to all the things that we talked about and all the things we did. Do they no longer exist too?

CHAPTER 49

Two cops were talking to Mr. Pacheco. He was no longer wearing mirrored sunglasses and his hair was dripping wet. One of the cops leaned in close to him and said, "I am so sorry, Manny." The paramedics took Man's body away on a stretcher. His face present, placid and so full of sorrow that he looked like the face of Christ on the cross. Mrs. Pacheco walked into the backyard with Man's little brother. She wore a yellow dress and a white wide brimmed hat with daisies attached to it, so sunny, her attire in contrast with what had happened, it almost made me laugh. The boy looked curious; he was fully engaged with what was going on, yet holding tightly to his stepmother's hand.

Mrs. Pacheco let go of the boy's hand, went to Mr. Pacheco and put her arm around her husband. A police officer asked her if she was the one who called emergency. She looked at him for a few seconds, as if she didn't understand the question, and then shook her head ever so slightly. Mom stepped forward and said it was she who had called.

The cop walked us a few feet away from the Pacheco's. "How did you know to call?"

"My son saw Manuel in the pool, we live a couple houses down and he has a perch in the tree in the backyard, and binoculars, and he just, he just…" She started to cry.

The cop leaned down to me. His breath smelled like cigarettes, and it made me wretch.

"Tell me, son, what did you see?"

I wanted to comfort my mom. I had rarely seen her cry.

It disturbed me. Maybe more than anything else, even Man's death. Man's murder. Even though Mr. Pacheco was a few feet away, talking to the other cop, I had the feeling he could hear our conversation. Because I could hear his. I wanted to say I saw Mr. Pacheco hold Man's head underwater. But then I remembered all I saw was him putting his hand on top of Man's head and pushing him down. I didn't see more than that. But I knew he had killed Man.

"Son, can you please tell me what you saw?"

I couldn't get any words out. Didn't know exactly how to state what I saw. I heard Mr. Pacheco explaining to the other cop that Man didn't know how to swim, and he couldn't understand why he went into the pool, with all his clothes on. The cop said, "He must have fallen in."

I told the cop in my quiet voice, "I saw Man jump in and start sinking to the bottom, I thought he was drowning, because he had told me that he didn't know how to swim, but then something happened, he started wiggling, and he made his way to the side of the pool and grabbed hold, and managed to lift his head above the water, and then that's when I saw Mr. Pacheco come, and put his hand on Man's head." The cop looked up from writing in his notepad, he showed no emotion but there was something in his eyes- shock, awareness, but it quickly went away, and he was blank again. Blank and yet I could see the machinations of his brain, as if remembering that he was a cop, or remembering he was Mr. Pacheco's friend, or that Mr. Pacheco was a cop and cops don't kill their own children, they don't kill their own son, but then remembering somehow Mr. Pacheco's former wife had been killed, with a gun, and everyone knew Mr. Pacheco had done the killing, and killing your wife is one thing but killing a little boy another. I saw all that flash in that cop's face. Or that's what I thought he would be thinking.

"Are you sure that's what you saw?" the cop asked me. I nodded my head. The cop walked away toward the other cop talking to Mr. Pacheco. And I heard him say that Mr. Pacheco found Man at the bottom of the pool, jumped in, pulled him out and tried to revive him, but it was too late. The boy had drowned.

"Come here, GG," Mom said and put her arm around me. As we moved to leave, the cop who had been talking to us said they would contact us for an official statement.

We walked back to our house. She held my hand. "Is that what you saw, GG? Did you see Mr. Pacheco try to kill Manuel?"

I nodded my head. "He didn't try. He did."

"I knew that there was something wrong with that man."

"That's not all," I said. And then I told her what Man had told me about seeing his dad kill his mother.

Mom laid with me in my bed that night. I couldn't stop crying. Not a loud, tearful weeping, but a steady, mournful, cascading sorrow. She rocked me back and forth like I was a baby. And as she did, every now and then a big tear would splash against my face or arm. One of her big, potent tears.

What does it mean to die? Man's body is still here, or there, or somewhere. They took it away. That was Man. That was his body. That was him. What makes him dead? What makes him no longer Man? Is it because his heart no longer beats? His father held him down underwater, and so after a while Man could no longer breathe, and if you don't breathe, that somehow stops your blood from receiving oxygen and so it stops flowing from your heart; your heart stops beating, and so you die. But what about your brain? Your brain, where you do all the thinking, where you think about the things that make you happy or sad, the brain where your memories are kept. Man had so many bad memories. Do they now go away? Is he free from them now? Or is his brain the only thing that is still working? Not his body anymore. But the brain needs the blood to be flowing to it. That's the source of energy. And so, it will stop working like the rest of Man. But what about the soul? And this is the thing Man told me about. The soul, the thing that is you, the thing that causes you to be you, that is not part of your body but is the thing that is the life force, the thing that when you die goes to heaven or hell depending on, depending on, well, according to Aunt Carmen, depending on whether or not you believe in Jesus Christ, and so even if you were a bad person you go to heaven. Man—he was a good person, I know he was a good person, but he told me himself that he didn't believe in Jesus Christ and the only reason he wore that cross around his neck was because his father forced him to. And he hated it. So, if the good people who don't believe in Jesus Christ go to hell and the bad people, the violent people like Mr. Pacheco, who believe in Jesus Christ, they go to heaven, well then, hell would be a safe place to spend eternity. And all of this kind of made me laugh. But my mom thought that I was crying, and she said, "There, there."

CHAPTER 50

She held me like the pieta Man had told me about. The door to my bedroom slowly opened. My father stepped in, put his hand on Mom's shoulder and said in a hushed tone that the police were there. They wanted to talk to her. I pretended to be asleep so Mom would feel okay leaving me.

Once I was sure that they had gone to the living room, I walked out of my room, being as quiet as I could. I passed the TV room where Kenny was watching a show. As I passed, he saw me but didn't say anything. I could see on his face he knew about what had happened and that he felt sorry for me. I went to the laundry room, which adjoined the kitchen, which was connected to the dining room. And there at the dining room table were two cops and my parents sitting across from them.

I stood completely still and listened to the conversation. It occurred to me that I had spent many moments in my life in the act of focusing my hearing over short distances to eavesdrop on grown-ups. This act of surveillance was for the purpose of attaining some sort of comprehension as to the motives and rationale for their behavior. I was never able to wrap my head around it. The cop asked my mom to please tell him why it was, or how it happened to be, that she called the emergency line.

"I was in the kitchen and my son came in, my youngest son, Gerald, and he said he had seen Manuel in his swimming pool, and he had seen the boy's father put his hand on the child's head, holding him down, and for me to call for help. There is a perch he built in the rubber tree out back and he sits up there with his binoculars; he says he watches the oil tanks a few blocks away so if there is a fire he can alert the Fire Department. He wants to be either a fireman or a forest ranger when he grows up. Well, that's what he's been saying. It didn't occur to me he was, well, kind of looking into other people's backyards."

"What exactly did he see?" the cops asked her. "I would rather not have to question the boy."

"He told me he saw Manuel and his father arguing, and then his father left, and he saw Manuel jump into the swimming pool, which was odd because Manuel had told him he didn't know how to swim."

"I see."

"But then he said he thought Manuel, well, he thought he may have been trying to kill himself. Because he couldn't swim. Why else would he jump into the swimming pool? But then Manuel started to flail around and made it to the side of the pool; he thought he decided he didn't want to die after all. And then he saw Mr. Pacheco walk over and put his hand on Manuel's head and pushed him under water."

"Did he actually see the boy's father hold him down underwater?"

"He said he saw him put his hand on Manuel's head and push him down beneath the surface of the water. That's when he ran to me, to have me call emergency."

The second cop wrote what Mom was saying in his notebook.

"Are you going to have to talk to my son? Is he going to have to testify in court?"

"No, that won't be necessary. We have determined that the cause of Manuel's death was accidental drowning; his father was just trying to rescue him. That's what your son saw. Manuel had drowned, possibly a suicide though we won't call it that. By the time Mr. Pacheco got to him it was too late."

"But that's not what my son saw."

"He's just a boy, ma'am. Sometimes imaginations get away

with themselves."

That's when I came out. "But that's not what happened!" I cried.

Mom motioned to me. I climbed on her lap. The cop said, "All right, son. Tell us what happened." And I pretty much repeated what my mom had said.

The cop looked at me sympathetically and asked, "Now, why would he want to kill his own son?"

"Because Man saw him shoot and kill his mom."

"Is that what Manuel told you?"

"Yes."

"Mrs. Pacheco's death was a tragedy. But it wasn't Manuel's father who killed his mother; it was Manuel. By accident. He had got hold of Officer Pacheco's revolver and it discharged, killing his mom. Forensics determined this; Manuel's fingerprints were all over the gun."

"I don't believe it," I said.

"I'm sorry, son. I don't think Manuel ever recovered from the guilt of it, which is why he tried, why he killed himself."

I stared at the cop, coldly, with hatred in my body. Mom took me out of the room and led me back to my bedroom. She pulled out pajamas from my dresser. I took them and went into the bathroom to put them on and brush my teeth. I looked into the mirror. Bloody Mary, Bloody Mary, Bloody Mary.

Mom tucked me in. I signaled her with my eyes to lay down next to me, which she did. She put her arm around me and kissed my forehead. "Some things we can never know for sure, my GG. Just try to put it out of your head for now, my darling." She stroked my hair, and I fell asleep. We didn't say the prayer about if I should die before I wake.

CHAPTER 51

The weather, the air, the temperature barely changes. Most of the time. Though, sometimes the wind makes the difference. The Santa Ana winds. And when the Santa Ana winds are strongest, it is a sign, it is a signal that autumn is coming. These devil winds make the smog, the ever-present smog, much more stultifying. According to National Geographic magazine katabatic winds exacerbate brush and forest fires, and ironically causes hotter temperatures along the coast, more so than in the desert.

The Santa Ana Winds caused my brother to have a serious sinus condition which required him to go to the doctor. The doctor drained his nasal passageways with a small balloon and put him on antibiotics. He lay on the sofa for two days, mummified in a purple and yellow appliqué quilt my Nana had made; more sedentary than ever I could remember him.

And then the winds gave way to another Southern California phenomenon, the Santa Ana fog; a sudden transition of hot dry air to cool, moist marine weather. It was as if a massive spirit had taken possession of the neighborhood. It happened in a flash.

Quite early one morning, having just taken our dog Clive for a walk, I stood motionless on the lawn of our house; thoughts, images, words immersed me into a trance-like state, my vision transfixed on the stillness before me. I saw an enormous fluffy white caterpillar languidly making its torpid way down my street. I remained where I was. Straight away I was enveloped in it.

School resumed. I went into the fifth grade. I remembered what Man had told me: "Don't say anything to anyone." He was talking about the things that he had told me. But I took what he said, I took it to mean something more. And so, I stopped talking altogether. The teachers and my parents got concerned. I was always on the quiet side, especially compared to Kenny, but for a kid to stop talking completely, especially considering what I had recently gone through, it was odd, and disturbing; more disturbing for them than for me.

I knew if I did speak, I would speak about what I knew to be true. Man's father had killed Man's mom, had killed Hector, and had killed Man. What was the use of speaking if you told the truth about the most important thing in the world- nobody believed you, or if they did believe you, they wouldn't do anything about it?

Since I loved Harpo Marx so much, I, copying him, was good at expressing myself with frowns, smiles, shrugs, and a little pantomime.

After a few weeks they brought me in to talk to a thera-pist. Since I wasn't speaking, there was only so much that he could gather from me. His name was Mr. Spengler. He was, I think, about twenty-five years old, had medium length blonde hair and an earnest face which allowed a kid to feel at ease in his presence. It seemed he was not so far removed from being a kid himself. He told me to call him Michael, but I didn't call him anything.

We sat in his little room, the little room they had given him, formerly a utility room, and we played Jenga. We played Jenga and he would ask me questions, to which I replied with a shrug or nod. I understood that the idea with Jenga was to keep my hands busy so I could answer him without thinking about how I would answer. To answer him automatically. He would ask things about how my life was at home. He asked me about my father. If he was nice to me. My father wasn't home for dinner every night, not like he used to be, and I thought about the phone call that I had answered, from his "girlfriend." Even if I was willing to talk, what would I say about it? And with all the stuff going on about Man, I had put that out of my mind. But Dad was nice when he was home, nice to me, and so I nodded. He asked if I got along with my brother. I shrugged. The truth was, we got along better than ever. We never fought anymore. My brother just looked at me like I was some sort of wounded bird.

Mr. Spengler asked if I was close to anyone. If I had any close friends. I shrugged. He must have known about Man. Mom probably told him.

He didn't ask a question concerning my mom. He just made a statement that the bond between a boy and his mom is special and that by talking to her he could tell how much she loved me. I stared at him. When he talked about my mom his eyes became incandescent, vulnerable. I leaned into him, I wanted to touch him, to take hold of his hand; he looked as if he might cry. We sat in silence for I don't know how long. "You're lucky to have such a nice mom, never take that for granted."

Finally, his serious demeanor broke and we went back to playing Jenga.

And what about my other family? My aunts and uncles and cousins. I shrugged.

"What does that mean? Those shrugs?" I shrugged again. "You do have cousins?" I nodded. "Do you see them very often?" I shrugged. We saw my cousins a lot during the summer, but we hadn't seen them since my birthday. And I missed my cousins. They were fun and listened to good music, especially Cousin Cassandra. But my parents no longer went out and so Cassandra didn't come over to babysit, probably because my mom didn't want to leave me alone, but also because my parents didn't seem like they were in the mood to go to any movies. There was something going on between them. They didn't seem happy.

The other kids in school also looked at me funny. Wounded bird. I guess they heard about Man. It was a big news story on the television.

I still saw Mr. Pacheco every day when I came home from school. He was either mowing his lawn or doing yardwork, tending to his roses with pruning shears in a gloved hand. They had placed him on bereavement leave but he didn't seem like a man who was much bereaved.

We continued with the therapy sessions every day during recess while the other kids were playing.

CHAPTER 52

One night, after my bath, sitting in the living room; Mom sewing buttons on various articles of clothing, a semi-annual occasion, Kenny reading William Shirer's Rise and Fall of the Third Reich, and I reading the book Man had given me. Dad came home. He tripped on the lip to the living room. He stopped, regained his balance and looked at us looking at him and sang, "Hello, I must be going, I cannot stay. I came to say I must be going. I'm glad I came but just the same I must be going." He chuckled, dropped his briefcase, and walked up to Mom's chair. He leaned down, "Hello there." He gave her a kiss and then stood back up. "I know what you're thinking. I know what you're thinking. Just a couple beers is all. That's all. And why not. And maybe a martini, or two." He looked at Kenny and me. "Boys. Sometimes you just have to cut loose. There is justice and then there is justice denied. Too often. Too often."

"I saw it on the news Dad. I can't believe it."

"Well, just goes to show. Sometimes. People get away with murder."

"It's like if they let Charles Manson go free." Kenny said disgustedly.

"Yes. Something like that," Dad said.

"Well, now," Mom said, "Let's not exaggerate. I believe that pardoning Nixon might be the best and easiest way to put the whole ugly mess behind us."

"No! Not true. Not true at all. You, my darling wife, are too kind. You are too sweet and too forgiving. You are much too forgiving."

"That might be true," she said and then went back to sewing buttons back on shirts that had probably been out-grown anyway.

CHAPTER 53

My grandparents started housesitting. It was a way to make a little money. They were sitting at a nice place in Santa Barbara. My parents and I went to spend the night with them. Kenny was on a Boy Scout trip.

The house had a flat roof and was surrounded by eucalyptus trees. The smell of the trees filled the air, it reminded me of Vicks vapor rub. There were plants everywhere and ferns in pots hanging from macramé throughout the place. The light in the place was diffused by windows that had a slight golden tint on them. Everything had an amber glow.

At dinner that night, Mom was drinking a fair amount of white wine. She had been a bit addled since the day that Man died. It was noticeable, as was the tension between my father and her. To make conversation my grandfather brought up the new television show, Chico and the Man. Mom glared and said she hated the show. Chico was a ridiculous stereotype. It wasn't how Mexicans really were, but how they were portrayed all the time in television and films, in that exaggerated way, she hated it. My father seemed uncomfortable. Usually, it was he who made such opinionated declarations. And the more wine she drank, the more vehement she sounded. Grandpa was defensive. Not so much of the show, but of the right of writers and creators to characterize ethnicity, and in many ways, this was the basis of a lot of comedy he said. And a lot of the things that are part of the stereotype are based in reality. "Look at our gardener, for instance. He never trims the hedge, even though it's his job." The room was quiet. "I'm joking," he said. Even though he wasn't joking entirely.

Mom lost her temper. "Now I know how you really see me." The room got quiet. I looked around at the faces. My father looked at Mom, not mad, confused; how she was behaving wasn't computing with the way she normally behaved.

My grandfather's expression was strained. Like his head might explode. His ears were red and his eyes wide. "Eat your peas sweetie," Nana told me.

I sat dumbstruck. Mom threw down her napkin, got up and went out to the porch, slamming the door. My grandfather shook his head as if to snap out of something, a bad dream, and said, "I didn't mean anything by it." He got up from the table and went into the living room. Nana started cleaning the table and then doing the dishes. Just my dad and I still sitting at the table. He was looking at the wine in his wine glass. He took a sip and looked at me and shrugged. Mom came back in and walked past us and went into their bedroom.

"Let's go for a walk," Dad said.

As we walked around the neighborhood he told me, "You know, son, sometimes people say things, and either they get misconstrued, or they don't mean to hurt someone's feelings, but they just don't know there are things that what they are saying might be hurtful to the person they were talking to. Maybe a person's experiences in life had made them sensitive about certain things. My father, your grandpa, is a good man. He is a very good man. He just comes from a different time. But he has spent his life always doing the right thing. He worked hard at his job, and he supported Nana and me, paying for everything even when times were tough. In those days the wife didn't work, and so that part was all on the man. And he was always, I don't know, just always faithful." At this point, I couldn't tell, but it seemed like he was crying. He took off his glasses and wiped his eyes. "But he's a good man."

We got back to the house. My father went into the bedroom to be with my mom. I hung out in the living room where Nana was. She was watching a detective show on television. She smiled at me and said, "Seems like it is always you and me left watching the shows." I went over and gave her a hug. She patted my head.

I got up to go to the bathroom. I passed my grandparents' bedroom; the door was slightly open, and I could see my grandpa sitting in a chair in the dark room. I went up to him. He was crying. "I am a bad man, So stupid. Don't be like me GG."

I didn't say anything. I took his hand and kissed it. He looked down at me and smiled. "You're a good boy. Don't worry, everything is going to be all right. I didn't mean anything by it. I love your mother dearly. We are all doing the best we can. I just don't know anymore. I just don't know, what is the right thing to say. But you must learn from mistakes; that's maybe the most important thing in life."

The next day at breakfast, nobody talked about what had happened the night before. Everyone was bright and cheerful. The breakfast was bountiful, fresh rolls that Nana made, potato gratin and scrambled eggs with green onions that Dad made, pancakes that Mom took care of, and fresh-squeezed orange juice by way of Grandpa.

"These oranges come right from their backyard. Wouldn't that be nice to have your own orange tree?" he said laughing.

"Sure would," Mom said gaily.

I didn't understand how they could be so happy, like what had happened the night before hadn't happened at all. I was partly disturbed by that and by what had happened, but also relieved at this performance of normalcy. I was also very hungry; I hadn't eaten dinner because of all the tumult.

CHAPTER 54

eet me at the hideout. Said the words written in blue ink on a folded piece or yellow construction paper, which I found on my desk after therapy with Mr. Spengler.

I got home, fixed myself a glass of Ovaltine, drank it down quickly, ran out of the house, and got my bike from the back of the garage. I had to pass the Pacheco house on the way to the lot. I didn't have to pass it. I could have gone the other way; it would be out of my way, but at least I wouldn't have to see that house, the house where Man was killed. But I wanted to see it. I wanted to show, at least to myself, that I wasn't afraid, wasn't afraid of evil. But, I was afraid, yet that didn't stop me from passing by the house.

Mr. Pacheco popped out from behind a car parked on the street, grabbed my handlebar, took a furtive look around, and then told me, "If you ever breathe a word about Manny's crazy idea that I had something to do with his mother's death, then I will do something terrible. I promise you. You love *your mother*, you told me, you love her so much, like Manuel loved his mother. If you cross me, not only will I kill your mother, but I will do terrible things to her before I do?" I looked at him, trying to control my terror, to not give in to his brutality. If I didn't register it, absorb it, it might cease to exist. And then he explained to me what rape was. The tears started then. "And then I will kill her, and then I will kill you and your whole goddamn family, and I will make it look as if it was the work of the Suburban Killer. Because that's what he does. I should just kill you now. But I think that you love your mother enough that you won't do anything stupid."

When I got to the enclave Kathy could tell I was shaken. She couldn't know what had just transpired between Mr. Pacheco and myself, but she did know all that had happened. We sat and stared out at the rocks and dirt until it was time to go home for dinner.

CHAPTER 55

More and more Dad was missing dinners. And when he did come home, it was after we were all in bed. He said that he had been very busy with new clients, and he had joined the Kiwanis Club. They had events during the week. Mom never said anything about it. At least not in front of us.

One night I heard him come home. It was late. I heard my parents talking in the kitchen. I snuck around to the laundry room.

"He just ran out into the street. There was nothing I could do."

"Was he killed?" my mother asked.

"No, I don't think so. I stopped just in time. He was on drugs or something. He was wearing an army jacket. Maybe a vet."

"Were you drinking?" And it was quiet for a minute.

"No. But I could use a drink now." And I heard him open the liquor cabinet door and then make himself a drink.

"Are you alright?" Mom asked him.

"Yes. I am."

"Here," she said. I peeked around the corner and saw them hugging. And I saw, for the second time in my life, my father crying.

I had another strange dream that night. Jesus was standing over me, and there was light coming through the holes in his hands. He had a long beard and long hair, but his face was

Man's. The blood from his hand was dripping on me. I shouted, "Leave me alone!"

CHAPTER 56

I went over to Greg's house. Rang the bell. His mom answered. She looked tired. Even her smile was tired. She was the same age as my mom, but she looked about ten years older. "He's in the garage, of course." Her words were a little slurred. "That's where they go." She studied me. "You're a nice boy." I nodded. "Things are changing so much. This country is almost unrecognizable to what it was when I was growing up. You should have seen it then. So much nicer." She gazed at me. "Not nicer, No, that's not the right word. So much more- hospitable."

Greg was looking into a microscope. He looked up and saw me. "Hey Gerald. Your mom does this for a living, doesn't she?" I nodded. "Still not talking, eh?" I nodded. "I cut my finger." And he held up a bandaged forefinger. "So, I put the blood on a slide, and I've been checking it out. Wanna look?" I nodded and went over to the microscope. "They look like little doughnuts. That's a high-powered microscope. I won't tell you where I got it, but it's not a toy or anything." He was right. They looked like little doughnuts.

I stopped looking at the microscope and sat down on the stool beside where he was standing. "So, Gerald, why did you stop talking?" I shrugged. "I think you saw something, but that didn't make you stop talking. But you saw what happened to Man. Didn't you?" I looked at him for a few seconds and then nodded. "But that's not why you stopped talking. You stopped talking because you told grown-ups what you saw, but they didn't believe you. That's why you stopped talking, right?" I stared at his face; at the way he was figuring everything out. I shook my head. "You stopped talking because you are afraid, you are afraid of what will happen to you if you talk." I could feel my face turning red. And tears swelling in my eyes. "You are afraid of Mr. Pacheco. You're afraid that if you talk, then what happened to Man will happen to you." I shook my head. "No? I thought you were afraid of Mr. Pacheco, yes?" I nodded. "So, you're not afraid that he will do something bad to you, but that he will do something bad to someone else if you talk about what you know, what you saw, and probably what Man told you. You're afraid that he will do something bad to your mom." I nodded as tears fell from my eyes. "Did he tell you; did he make that threat to you?" I nodded. "And he knows that he can get away with it, because he's a cop and he knows how to cover these things up. Cops get away with murder all the time. We have to do something." I shrugged. "Don't worry, I'll think of something."

"Have I ever told you my plan to rob a bank? It is much easier than you think. People get away with it all the time. You just need to find one, like right in the block of a busy city street, a few towns away from yours. You go there on a bike. And then you just need something that looks like a gun. You don't even need a real gun." He opened a drawer and pulled out a gun. It looked like the same cap gun that I had. It looked just like the guns you see on TV. I couldn't tell if it was real. "Find an alley, park the bike, make yourself into a lady; dress and wig and makeup and boobs, and you go in the bank and give the teller a note demanding money and flash the gun, and then you say if he sounds the alarm, you will blast him, you say you will blast him and anybody else that you see, so that it will be on his conscience if he does that. Who wants that on their conscience and who wants to die for someone else's money? Then you tell him to load a bunch of money on the counter and put it in the bag you set there and when he does you calmly walk away. You go to the alley where you parked your bike and take off the women's get up, put the money into a backpack, get on the bike and ride away. As a boy, not as a lady. I know what you're thinking. You're thinking that only an adult could pull something like that off. And maybe you're right. Whoever heard of a kid robbing a bank. But I could pass for a woman, and that's who they will be looking for. It's just a plan, a good plan, but it could work."

CHAPTER 57

My brother and I were eating at the kitchen counter watching the little portable television, which is where we ate when Dad didn't come home for dinner. We were eating Swanson's TV dinner, "Hungry Man". In the foil compartments there was a Salisbury steak in thick rust-brown onion gravy, hash brown potato nuggets, peas and carrots that looked like they had been made by a machine, and an apple cake concoction. Actually, it was quite delicious. Kenny started trashing me about not talking. "What's wrong with you? You think that you are Harpo Marx or something?" Mom told him to be quiet. Kenny snarked, "Things are weird enough, he doesn't need to be acting like a zombie. Everyone is always telling me how weird I am, Grandpa calls me motormouth, but at least I talk, and I am not some mute freak!"

Mom slammed a wooden spoon on the side of the counter, it broke and part of it went flying past Kenny, almost hitting his head. She held the other broken piece in her hand, looked at it and said mutedly, "I told you to please be quiet." She put it down and left the room.

We finished our dinners, put the empty foil containers in the trash, rinsed off our forks and the glasses, and then went into the TV room to watch the baseball game. After a while Mom came into the room. She seemed almost back to normal, and said, "It's time to get ready for bed."

I was sleeping when I heard a commotion in the living room. I thought that maybe it was my father coming home late, but the voice, a man's voice, wasn't my father's. And then I thought maybe it was Mr. Pacheco. I saw him in my mind, in our house, like a phantom. I heard footsteps coming down the hall, heading toward my brother's and my room. Then it stopped, the handle to our door started to turn. I heard my mother say, "No." The doorknob stopped turning.

I heard noises from the TV room across the hall. I thought that maybe my mother was in danger, but what could I do if it was Mr. Pacheco? He was so big and strong. But I had to do something. I got out of bed and went into the TV room holding my baseball bat. It was Uncle Dan folding out the sofa bed. "Hi, GG!" he said.

"Uncle Dan is going to spend the night inside. There's a bad storm coming." Mom said holding sheets. She gave me a look, tilted her head and looked at Uncle Dan who seemed to be struggling with the sofa bed. I put down the bat and went over and helped him pull it out.

The next morning, Mom made eggs and chorizo. Dad was there, and Uncle Dan, my brother and I, all having breakfast together, which was something that hardly ever happened anymore. Normally my father and Uncle Dan got along well, they both had a silly streak, but this morning there was tension, tension coming and going in both directions.

"So, Dan, where were you before the cop next door found you?"

Uncle Dan looked at my brother and me. "I went to Alaska. I went to Alaska to look for gold. It's true. First, I got a job on a fishing boat, salmon, and then when I got to Alaska, I had plenty of money, so much money. And I bought the stuff I needed to look for gold. You know, the pans and the heavy clothing, snow boots and a good backpack—you know, everything. But still it was so cold, so very cold. I thought that I could take it, but I couldn't. I stayed just outside of Fairbanks but only lasted a week! But I didn't want to come home broke, and so I went to gamble. If I turned my five thousand dollars into maybe one hundred thousand, and then when I came back Maria wouldn't think I was so crazy after all. There are these bingo parlors on the Indian reservation. I spent three days and nights; for three days I did not sleep. I gambled, and don't you know that I made one hundred thousand dollars, but then I had a bad streak and lost it all. I just had barely enough to get back to San Pedro. And there was the Dodge Dart station wagon, the one that your parents gave me, parked right where I left it. I slept for days. Quite an adventure."

"What about Maria? Have you spoken with her?" my father asked.

"Oh yes. She is very angry with me. But she loves me. Don't worry. I won't stay too long."

"Of course, you can stay as long as you need, Danny," Mom said.

"Gracias. I tried to make something good happen. To strike it rich. But sometimes it's just not in the cards. I can sleep outside again."

"Well, you are fine in the TV room. This rain is supposed to last for days. I hope that sofa bed isn't too uncomfortable, Danny," Dad said, trying to temper his tone and get some brownie points from Mom. Also, after all, he was fond of Uncle Dan.

"And since you work late so much, it is good that I am here. I can be of help, you know. These are strange and dangerous times in Southern California. A lot of freaks."

"Yes. Danny. There are a lot of freaks," Dad agreed.

CHAPTER 58

It was a Saturday. A very warm day in late September. We had the slip-and-slide going on in the front yard. The kids from the neighborhood were all playing on it. The Motley brothers, the Matz's, the Hanson brothers and Kathy Baker. I hadn't seen her since that day at the enclave. I thought she might be mad at me because she hadn't talked to me since. I did a big slide on my belly. Looked up and there was Kathy. She smiled down at me. Greg Gibson went down the slide, rolling over and over as he went. Seemed like he came out of nowhere as he wasn't there a minute before.

Kathy said to me, "Come on, let's go to the lot, to the enclave."

We started walking to the lot. We passed the Pacheco house. I knew what I would see because I could hear it; Mr. Pacheco pushing the lawnmower, terry-cloth shorts, sneakers, no socks, and no shirt, and those mirrored sunglasses. And that is exactly what I saw.

Kathy took my hand. "You've been through a lot, mister," she said to me. We walked along, and I took one last look over my shoulder. The lawnmower sputtered and stopped. Mr. Pacheco leaned over to see what was wrong, and the thing exploded. The explosion sent him flying backward. He lay on the ground, his body and clothes on fire. He was screaming like an animal. Screaming from somewhere deep in his body, a high pitch scream like a police siren gone awry. Troy and Rex Hanson came running over from my yard. Troy grabbed the hose and Rex turned it on. They worked in tandem almost like they had rehearsed this moment. Troy doused Mr. Pacheco's body, and the fire went out. Rex shouted, "Someone call an ambulance!"

CHAPTER 59

My mother stood over me, in her lab coat. Her head shrouded in fluorescent light. "Well, there you are," she said with a sweet, yet somewhat tortured smile. She touched my forehead and brushed aside my hair. "I think your football days are over my friend. Or better stick to flag football. How do you feel?" I felt dizzy and a little nauseous and had a headache, but I said, "Okay." The first words I had uttered since taking my vow of silence.

The kids in the neighborhood had decided to have a football game in the park. It was Sunday, a great football day in Southern California, where the hometown team, the LA Rams, were having a great season. We all followed the Rams. I wasn't as crazy about football as I was about baseball, but I liked it. All the boys in the neighborhood collected not only baseball cards but football cards as well. You'd go down to the convenience store with two dimes and get a pack of baseball and a pack of football cards. Watching these giant men clash on the television sets, like warriors, and hearing the grown men watching and yelling at every brutal tackle or touchdown, there was something about it that brought you, as a kid, into the company of men; you felt more mannish simply by watching the game on television.

Playing in the park was another story. And it was one of those devil wind Sundays. It felt good to be playing, to be getting the football, breaking tackles, making touchdowns, making great catches at the end zone. And with my Cullen Bryant white and blue jersey, I fantasized that I was on the Rams.

My brother was quarterback as usual. Calling all sorts of fancy plays. When we played football, it was one of the rare times that he and I worked well together. In the huddle he called for a double fake. Kenny knelt behind the center. He called out a bunch of numbers: "21, 44, 68, 22, hut, hut, hut, hike." He took the ball, backed up, faked a throw to the wide receiver, who cut across in front of the offensive line, then faked a handoff to the full back, who pretended that he had the ball and ran down the field, and then he did a flea flicker to me. I ran towards the end zone—there was nobody there on that side and so I had it free and clear—but out of nowhere, like a blur, I saw him out of the corner of my eye, a black ghost, plowed into me- hard, brutally. I lost consciousness.

Mom told me that I had a mild concussion and that I had a broken knuckle. My right hand, which was now in a cast. Which was fortunate since I was left-handed. Nobody else in the family was. It was a topic of discussion; how I was the only left-handed person in the entire family. "When can I go home?" I asked. Mom said that we could leave after she finished her shift, which ended at 3 o'clock. But then she did a double take. "GG. You spoke." I nodded.

They put me in a wheelchair, standard procedure. No one was allowed to walk out of the hospital. They didn't want to be liable in case someone fell. Even if they seemed able to walk under their own powers. The orderly explained this to me. Mom walked alongside us. The orderly was a young, cheerful woman. She was telling me what a nice person my mother was. I told her that I knew that, and they both laughed.

"Anita." We stopped. It was Beth, one of her fellow lab technicians. I had seen her and her husband a few times at the parties at our house and the parties that they hosted. They had a nice swimming pool, and coincidentally, a daughter my age and a son my brother's. She looked at me and pointed to my cast. "Hello Gerald. I heard you had a little football injury. Guess you'll have to wait a while before trying out for the Rams." I smiled and said, "I like baseball better anyway."

As they chatted, I noticed that we were near the emergency section. I barely remembered coming in through that area. Vague memories of being in an ambulance and then being transferred to a gurney. I looked and saw that we were standing right next to the intensive care unit, and through an open door, on a bed, was a man with all sorts of tubes going in and out of his body, out of his mouth, out of his nose. He was wrapped like a mummy. I knew it was Mr. Pacheco.

CHAPTER 60

I didn't think that you were ever going to talk again,"

"Me either."

"What made you decide to start talking?"

"When my mom asked me how I was, in the hospital, I just automatically said that I was okay. I guess I didn't want her to worry."

Kathy and I were in the clubhouse on the side of the house. After school. Dad was at work and my brother was playing Anzio with Doug in the dining room. I figured we could hang out there safely without being disturbed.

"That was insane, what happened to Man's dad. I wonder if he is going to live," Kathy said.

"Yeah. I saw him in the hospital. He is hooked up to all sorts of machines. Maybe he is going to die. I don't know. He was burned all over his body."

"Do they know how it happened?" she asked, as if I knew.

"I don't know."

"Well, I am sure glad it did. He was scary, especially after what Man told me."

"Man told you...?" I said, totally surprised.

"Yeah. About him seeing his dad shoot his mom."

"Oh. That's weird. I thought I was the only one he told. Besides Hector"

"He said that I was the only other person he told. Except you and Hector."

"Hector is dead."

"I know."

She touched my hand lightly. I got a shock from static electricity, she did too. We laughed. Somehow, for a few seconds, getting electrocuted, just a little bit, by another person, was the funniest thing in the world. Then she got serious and said,

"Do you want to kiss?"

"Yes."

"That's good. I thought that you would never kiss me again."

"I like you. I like your eyes."

"You like my eyes!" she said and snickered. "What about them do you like?"

"They're bright and fearless."

"Thanks. I like your eyes too. They are dark and scared, but very beautiful."

And then we kissed.

The Angels were beating the Cleveland Indian five to zero. Nolan Ryan was pitching a gem. He had given up just one hit through five innings. He struck out the side in the top of the sixth. A commercial came on for Alka-Seltzer which was funny but not as funny as Kenny was making out. He looked at me with a decidedly crooked expression. And then I heard my voice say, "I like you. I like your eyes." And then Kathy saying, "You like my eyes!" He pulled out his yellow Panasonic portable tape player. The thought quickly ran through my mind, he had recorded the whole conversation, including that part about Man's father killing his mom. "I like your eyes," he said, mimicking me, and started laughing hysterically.

A strange kind of anger possessed me. I jumped on him, knocking the tape recorder off the sofa as the rest of Kathy and my conversation played. I grabbed his shoulder and wrestled him to the ground, and then I started shaking him furiously, his head striking the carpeted floor and bouncing back up repeatedly. And then I was outside myself, looking down at myself attempting to kill my brother. I raised the arm with the cast, to slam it on his skull, to crush his skull, I could see it crack and blood and brains spilling all over the rust brown carpet.

I rolled off him. He lay there, not moving. And I thought I might have possibly killed him. "Kenny, Kenny. Are you okay?" He was motionless. "I better go get Mom," I said.

He started moving. "No. Don't. You stupid jerk."

And then such a feeling of remorse and shame came over me. And like a bolt of lightning it hit me and illuminated this thing inside me, this thing that was inclined to cause suffering and harm to others, and this light, it went through me, and even though I felt such shame for how I had hurt and could have possibly killed my brother, I also felt relief because I knew that going forward, not only would I never do violence again, but there was something inside me, a mechanism, that would prevent it. At least, that is what it felt like in that moment and it was I hoped. With all my might.

CHAPTER 61

I looked out at the oil tanks, and then at Man's backyard, and the pool where he died. So tranquil and clean and blue- blue like Listerine, blue like the sky at the beach at noon, blue like my grandfather's eyes, blue like Dodger blue, blue like this feeling inside of you.

A man in white coveralls came out through the screen door and into the backyard. He lit a cigarette, a few short quick puffs and then a long inhale followed a slow exhale of light gray smoke. He had a strong build and dark hair. At first, I thought it was Mr. Pacheco. But then I saw it was a younger man. Mrs. Pacheco came out. The man threw the cigarette to the ground and stepped on it with his white sneaker. Mrs. Pacheco gave him a look of consternation and began speaking with urgency. And then they both went inside.

Something happened in the sky. A loud booming sound: one, two, three. Three times. Louder than anything that I had ever heard. I thought that it was the oil tanks blowing, yet no sign of smoke that way, and then I thought that perhaps this was it, this was the atomic attack, this was the nuclear war that we had all grown to accept was inevitable, that finally the Russians were dropping their megaton bombs. This was the end of civilization.

I ran inside the house, but there was nobody there. It was Saturday and I remembered that my parents were at couples' therapy, which they had just started, but my brother, who was supposed to be watching me, was nowhere to be found. I ran out of the house and went to Greg Gibson's house. Greg was in his front yard, just standing there.

"What is it?" I asked him.

"No, Gerald, it is not a nuclear war. Those were sonic booms. Jets, going faster than the speed of sound; I guess three of them. When something breaks the speed of sound, it creates enormous amounts of sound energy." He put his hand on my shoulder. "So, you're talking again." I nodded. "Just supersonic aircraft, Gerald. Nothing to be afraid of."

Sometimes I thought of Greg as a grown man, even though he was only thirteen, and sometimes I thought of him as a kind of Huckleberry Finn character as there was something about him that was like he came out of a book. He wore prescription safety glasses with one of its stems held in place with a safety clip. He had sandy blonde hair of medium length that usually looked like it hadn't been washed for a while. And most often he was wearing soiled and smudged baby blue coveralls that seemed like they hadn't been washed in a while; much too large, rolled up at the sleeve and ankles with a blue patch that said DuPont above the left breast.

I didn't ask him whether he had anything to do with Mr. Pacheco's lawn mower exploding. I didn't have to. I wondered if the police had found any evidence linking him with the incident. But there he was, in the flesh. Seemingly unworried about anything. Not at all carrying any remorse or regret. He knew that Mr. Pacheco was a killer, and a threat to me and my family, and so he did something about it because nobody else would. And even though I was against violence, I, was glad that he had.

I had often asked myself what I would have done if I was a young man and it was World War II, and I knew that Hitler was murdering Jews by the millions—how could I not go and to try to stop him, even if that meant killing others and possibly getting killed myself? Mr. Pacheco was a killer too. And so even though I wasn't sure it was Greg who made the lawnmower explode, I knew it was, and I was grateful to him for it.

But my Uncle Dan and Joshua and cousins Chris and

John were not killers, not like Hitler and Mr. Pacheco. But they killed, probably killed many people, probably some women and children. They did so because their country asked them too. They believed that their country wouldn't ask unless there was a righteous reason. Because their country was holy, ordained, moral. They were under the impression that they wouldn't be asked to go to Korea or Vietnam to kill unless there was a good reason, and they accepted the reason their country gave them. In Mr. Pacheco's mind, did he have a moral imperative to kill? He must have. Why else would he kill his own son?

CHAPTER 62

I t felt safe under there; anonymous, clean, just two holes so that I could see. With a white sheet over my head, I felt like a witness; I was a witness, a secret, not-so-secret witness. I had seen and heard many things, many terrible things.

Kenny was dressed as Richard Nixon with a Richard Nixon mask, frumpy suit, and an empty bottle of Jack Daniels in his pocket. Dad dressed as Groucho Marx of course. With his bushy mustache and cigar, he didn't take much fixing up. Mom had on a simple witch costume, black hat, and a dress. She looked very pretty, and she seemed happy, cautiously happy.

My father and mother sent us off into the night, waving from the porch where they would be stationed to hand out candy. I turned to look at them as we made a left from the driveway, and I saw them kiss. A long, loving kiss, something I hadn't seen in a long time. That buoyed my spirits right away because I felt connected to my mother; everything I was feeling, she felt, I knew this intrinsically.

And in turn, everything she felt, I felt. Or at least, I conjectured what those emotions meant, seeing them, as she projected with her expression and body language, and then feeling them, as they inhabited my body and space.

At first, I did not want to participate in Halloween. And said as much. It all seemed too disturbing on every level. Kathy tried to talk me into it. But I was resistant. And even my brother, who hadn't spoken to me since the incident with the tape recorder, encouraged me to take part. "It wouldn't be the same without you," he told me begrudgingly, and that made me feel like he wasn't mad at me anymore, and maybe I could forgive myself for getting so violent with him. But I could not think of what to go as.

One night I had a dream. In the rubber tree, a telescope pointed at black and purple clouds in the sky. I was not ten years old; I was older. I had a mustache. And very long hair. A tap on my shoulder. In the yard. The horse pinata, massacred on the ground, blood and guts everywhere, it quickly reassembled itself and ran off, hopping over the backyard fence. Another tap on my shoulder. No longer older, I turned around. It was Man. He was in good spirits. "What are you going to do with that?" He asked me, pointing to the gun in my hand. "I don't know. Maybe kill your dad." He laughed and said, "Don't bother." He took the gun away from me, held it for a few seconds and it turned into a yellow number two pencil. He handed that back to me. I took it and held it up to my eye as if it were a telescope. "You should be a kid again," he told me. "But how can I?" I said, "After everything." He slowly became pale and transparent and said, "I don't know. Just by doing kid stuff."

I was jubilant to be eating candy. That was something that I hadn't done for a little while. It was something that I was depriving myself of. I no longer allowed myself to enjoy things like watching television, baseball, eating candy and ice cream. I just read a lot. And listened to records by the Beatles. But tugging on an Abba Zabba or biting into that nut right in the middle of an Almond Joy, or chewing a strawberry Starburst, or enjoying a multi-layered Milky Way; it was all so good. I could feel my body changing, and I felt like I was becoming something else. There, under that white sheet, I felt high and even invincible. Beneath the white sheet, I was anonymous, and in my mind the ghost of Man. Or it was like the ghost of Man had merged with my identity. And my wish was that Man could be amidst the children laughing and playing and with the parents so joyfully doling out the candy this idea was real in my mind. Everyone not only looked different because of the costumes, but they seemed different. It was like I had never seen so many happy people. It my way for Man to experience it, to be his ghost, I could be a vehicle for him, his soul could enter mine and he could taste the candy, be around the gaiety.

We had become a little group: Kenny, Kathy, dressed as a cowgirl, in ponytails, with cowboy hat, red vest with tassels, skirt with a cowhide pattern on it, and six shooter in a holster. The Motley brothers as assorted ghouls and Greg Gibson, dressed as a mad scientist, of course. Lab suit, hair all puffed out Einstein style and big black horn-rimmed glasses. He stood over us, not just because he was so tall and a little older, but because he, in my mind, was out protector. And he was a kind of celebrity. And here he was mingling with all the kids, something that I rarely saw him do. Not as the star, not as a munition's expert or stunt daredevil Evel Knievel trashcan jumper, but just as a kid, trick-or-treating.

The night sky was filled with stars, the air so cool and the smell of fireplaces burning wood, and the sweet smell of artificially fruit-flavored candy all mixed. How easy it was to slip back into being a kid again. Was it real?

We traversed most of our block and two other blocks to boot. And then we were back hitting the few houses we hadn't before. My bag, a plain white pillowcase, was getting filled up with candy. "Well, I'm going home." Greg said abruptly. "See ya Gerald." He clapped me on the back and left.

I said to Kathy, "That's my best friend."

She looked a little upset. "What about me?"

I made sure that no one was listening. "You're my girlfriend." She smiled. Kenny rang the doorbell of a new house. Then I realized what house it was. Whose house it was. But I felt that I could not move; my feet felt planted in the ground.

"Trick or treat!" the group sounded as the door opened. And there was Mrs. Pacheco, in the same witch hat and black dress as my mom, and she smiled, she smiled as if nothing had happened, as if Man hadn't been killed or Man's father hadn't been so seriously injured. She smiled as if she was possessed by something, not a scary smile, it was a beautiful, radiant smile, and as she handed out the candy. I could see she had a little bump on her belly.

Man's little brother, who was dressed as a fireman, was standing by her side, he didn't seem to be enjoying any of the festivities. And behind Mrs. Pacheco, in the living room, the place where Mr. Pacheco had once showed me his gun, the gun that had killed Man's mom, there he was, Mr. Pacheco, in a wheelchair, covered in bandages. The room was dark except for the light of a television set flickering, but I could see his face. The skin was red and frayed, and his head slumped. He looked dead, or half dead. So distracted by the sight of him I hadn't noticed that I had got pushed to the door.

"Why, who is this? It is a ghost I see, is it Casper the friendly ghost?"

I stood, not moving. "No, Mrs. Pacheco. I am not Casper. I am the ghost of Man. Manuel Pacheco."

And the weird thing was, she didn't stop smiling. It was like I hadn't said anything to her. All the kids were jabbering, so they hadn't heard me. But Kathy did, and she tugged my arm, and we left just as Mrs. Pacheco was about to put some candy into my pillowcase. The same pillowcase that I had slept on so many times dreaming about Man, hearing Man speak to me, from beyond, because he truly was beyond, beyond all of this. Was he eliminated when he died, did he have no spirit?

That was what my father believed: "When you're dead, you're dead." I had heard him say at dinners with friends, after some wine, proudly professing his atheism. Nobody taking exception. Nobody except my mom, who would simply say, "You don't know that. Some things you can't know."

CHAPTER 63

Her hair was jet black hair, piled high on her head and draping down in strands on either side. Her black dress formed a long V from her shoulders to midway to her torso exposing her ample bosom. She wore red lipstick that seemed to vibrate because of the poor reception we got from the TV antenna. And she was hilarious, the voice overs usually during the scariest parts of the movie. And then she'd announce a commercial break with another funny quip. She was more entertaining than the movie. Kenny and I weren't not really paying attention anyway, we were busy trading candies. He didn't like anything with coconut, and I didn't like caramel after eating a bunch of homemade caramel my dad had concocted for a dessert last Thanksgiving, later only to throw it all up.

I traded Kenny my 100 Grands, Big Hunks, Charleston Chews for his Almond Joys, Mounds, and Coconut Patties. He also gave me his Chick of Stix because I had more caramel candies than he had coconut candies.

I gathered some candy together to take to Uncle Dan. He was staying in his tent in the backyard again. He felt he was too much in the way in the TV room. But I think it was the sofa bed with the obtrusive springs that had caused him to move out back. I had heard him say as much to Mom one morning. He stayed in an army pup tent with a roll and a pillow. Official U.S. ARMY issued. He said that this is what he used in Alaska. I wondered if it was the same one he used in Korea. Korean War where he had seen plenty of action. Mom had alluded to it as a possible source of his mood disorder. She said he had seen things, and when he came back from the war, he was different. More extreme in his moods and yet successful as an insurance salesman. For a while.

I passed through the kitchen to get to the door which led to the backyard. There my mother and father were engaged in something serious. Candles burning between them on the dining room table where they were having a late dinner. Their voices low, monotone. I tried to sneak past, but my mother saw me and said, "Did you have fun, mi El Fantasma?" I stopped, momentarily confused, and then realizing she was calling me a ghost in Spanish, I said, "Si." I went over to her.

She leaned down and gave me a kiss. "And where are you going now?"

"I have some candy that I wanted to give Uncle Dan."

My father gave me a pat on my head and said, "He is not here GG."

"Did he leave? Did he go back to his family?"

"No," Mom said. "But Maria let him come to go trick-or-treating with the younger kids. You know Uncle Dan, just a kid at heart."

My father took a sip of the wine and then said, "If he could stay sober, then Maria might let him come back."

CHAPTER 64

I left my parents in their rarefied state of intimacy. I went out to the backyard to leave the candy for Uncle Dan in his pup tent already set up in the middle of the yard. It was a bit odd as he usually didn't put it up until he went to sleep. He usually kept it rolled together and stuck in the tool shed. But there it was.

"Uncle Dan. Uncle Dan." But no answer. I slowly unzipped the flaps and peeled them back. I looked inside. Empty. I crawled in. Pretty sparse in there except a sleeping bag, an wind up alarm clock, an army-issued flashlight, a battery lantern, a Bible open and in its sheaf, a knife marking the page. I turned on the flashlight and set the candy on his pillow. I picked up the bible. I put it near my nose. It smelled like dried leaves. I set it down. I picked up the knife. I removed it from its sheath and set the sheaf next to the bible on the bed. The knife had a wooden handle with grooves going around the circumference. The blade was about the size of my shoe, starting wide and then curving to a sharp point. I touched it with the tip of my forefinger. It pricked it and a few droplets of blood issued forth. I turned my finger upward so the drops wouldn't fall. I studied both the knife and the blood and then put the knife on the bed next to the sheath. I suck up the droplets of blood. I picked up the bible and read from the page where the knife had been. John 5:19 - *We know that we are the children of God, and the whole world is under the control of the evil one.* Someone wearing a wolf mask violently pushed aside the flaps of the tent and let out a loud howl.

It crawled into the tent and snatched the knife. It held it up to his face and let out another howl. I was so frightened that I thought I was going to pee my pants. My breathing got constricted. My hands that held the bible started to shake. The thing growled, a long angry growl. The wolfman dropped the knife on the blanket and started laughing. Uncle Dan took off the mask.

"Hello GG. Did I scare you?" I nodded, about to cry. "It's okay to be scared but never show it when you are under attack. Use it. Use the power that the fear gives you." He smiled at me. "What are you doing in here?"

"I wanted to leave you some candy."

"And the knife and the bible got your attention."

"Yes."

"Well, gracias." He sat down in front of me on his knees. He picked up the knife again and looked at it. "Do you know what this is?" I nodded my head. "It's a Kay Bar."

"A K Bar?"

"Known as a fighting and utility knife. As if fighting was not a utility." He was slurring his words a little. "Its primary purpose is for stabbing, you know, when you don't want to make a lot of noise by firing your weapon, bringing a lot of un-wanted attention—that's when you use the Kay Bar. But you could use it also to cut a birthday cake. I have done both with it. They gave it to me before going to Korea. I usually carry it with me. In Alaska, yes, where there are bears that will have you for lunch. It might come in handy. Here, I keep it by my bed. There are more dangerous things than bears in Southern California—there are serial killers. But don't be scared, GG. Don't be scared. Or be scared. You switch the c and a in scared and it spells sacred. I know you have seen a lot. I have seen a lot too."

He put down the knife and took the bible from me. *"And the whole world is under the control of the evil one.* That doesn't mean that we cannot live in love, light and righteousness. Just means that you must decide to. And that the power of evil to sway a man is powerful. You know that GG. You know that as well as anyone. But remember what Saint Augustine said, 'In remembering past joy we can hope for its return in the future, just as the remembrance of past sorrow instills in us the fear of impending disaster.' Ah man's dichotomy. In other words, don't forget your friend, and let his memory be both something to bring joy and a reminder to be vigilant against destructive forces."

He set the bible down next to the knife. Picked up the knife and put it back into its sheath. He ruffled my hair. "Thank you for the candy. Now go eat yours and enjoy yourself. You're only a kid once."

CHAPTER 65

The next day, over and through empty candy wrappers and crumpled beer cans which littered the sidewalk, I rode my bike to Kathy's house. Her older brother Chris, and her dad were working on the magnificent red Trans Am parked in the driveway. Kathy's dad, under the open hood, seemed to have made a complete recovery from his heart attack because he was yelling at Chris over the sound of the engine. Chris was behind the wheel, "Okay, press on the gas," Chris made the car rev, an enormous sound, the kind of sound that filled up the whole sky. It sounded like an army, or an angry beast. I stood there watching. "Okay," the father said. And Chris stopped revving. "Kathy!" he yelled. "Your friend is here."

They kept working on the car. I watched as I waited for Kathy, who seemed to be taking a long time. Every now and then her father would give me a dirty look. Eventually Kathy came out of the garage wheeling a bike. It was an old, beat up, red Schwinn cruiser. A boys bike not a girl's bike. Smiling, she said, "My brother gave me his old bike."

At the red stop light at Moody Street, waiting for it to change, we gave each other rapid fire glances. Funny glances, affectionate glances, empathetic glances.

When we got to the lot, we found it completely enclosed. FUTURE HOME OF ABC SUPERMARKET, read a sign hanging on the wire meshed fence. Cranes and tractors and construction workers were busy transforming our enclave and the rest of it into a supermarket! Already concrete was being poured. So quickly our sacred place was eliminated.

We looked at each other sadly and shrugged. Guess we will have to find a new place to be together. We thought it. Didn't say it. We had gotten to a point where we didn't need to speak. Where we could read each other's thoughts. We got onto our bikes and rode to El Dorado Park, which was a good half-hour bike ride away.

El Dorado Park has a big golf course, a duck pond, a large grove of eucalyptus trees and an old wood bridge covered in grass that went over a little creek that led to a pond. We laid our bikes down and went underneath the bridge. We sat with legs crossed.

"Do you feel sad about Man?" she asked.

"Yes. But also, no. But also, angry. I am so angry."

"Why do you say no?"

"It's almost like he was never here. But also like he is still here and never died."

"Yes. I know what you mean. I keep expecting him."

"Do you believe in ghosts?" I asked her.

"No."

"Me neither. Or maybe a little. I don't know."

"I believe in spirits though."

"What's the difference?"

"According to an episode of The Night Gallery, a ghost is this person who is supposed to be trapped and can't get into the other world, where a spirit is like the spirit of a person and you can feel them, you know, like in a gust of wind or a sound that you don't know where it came from. I feel my grandma's spirit all the time. Well, not all the time, but sometimes."

"Do you ever feel Man's spirit?" I asked.

"No. Not yet. It takes time. Takes more time, I think."

We sat and listened to the birds in the eucalyptus trees. "Do you want some bubblegum?" She nodded. I pulled out a pack of Bazooka from my pocket and handed her a piece.

We sat there chewing. "Want another piece?" I asked. She nodded, and we both put another piece of Bazooka Joe in our mouths. We did this a few times, scattering the wrappers on the ground before us without thinking twice. We sat making bubbles- big, big, bubbles. We did that until it started to get dark. Then got back on our bikes and rode home.

CHAPTER 66

My father started being home most nights, except Tuesday and Thursday when he had Kiwanis functions, fundraisers, and drinks with his fellow Kiwanians. Since the organization was civic in nature, that of helping children and addressing the needs of children in the community. Mom couldn't argue with that. Their last pancake feed raised thousands for the pediatric trauma center in Orange. She was quite proud of my father for his involvement. Up to his recent membership in the Kiwanis he had just been a lot of talk about the ills of society.

My father commenced firing up the gas-fueled fireplace on the weekend nights. Though there isn't much when it comes to seasons in Southern California, still, in November there is a bit of a change in the air. The light at twilight has a luminescent quality, a translucent aura. The heat lets up and the dryness diminishes. People grow sentimental as the stores start carrying holiday-themed items.

For Thanksgiving we would be hosting a big family gathering. Aunt Ruth, Cassandra, Sandy would be there as would be Uncle Dan, still living with us, his wife Maria, their children: John, Chris, Danny Jr., and Darlene. And from my father's side, my grandparents, Aunt Jessie and Uncle Ray, their son, Arnold, his wife, Ethel, their two kids, Simon and Janet, and Uncle Herman and Aunt Ozell.

Uncle Herman was the de facto patriarch of the family on my father's side. Herman, Jessie, and Nana were born in

St. Louis in quick succession shortly after their parents, my great grandparents, Peter and Elizabeth, had emigrated from what they called The Pale, an area between Poland and Russia. The persecution of the Jews was rough, the pogroms frequent. They were married and then bounced through Ellis Island to St. Louis, where a relative got them settled. They had the children and then Peter was hit and killed by a trolley car, and Elizabeth died of tuberculosis. Herman, only twelve, went to work and supported the family. Later, he made a killing buying and selling real estate in Southern California and helped my grandparents buy a house in Downey.

Dad made a giant turkey, Nana helped with the fixings, Aunt Maria brought her tamales and Mexican rice, Aunt Ruth brought enchiladas, Aunt Jessie brought pies and blintzes, and Mom made the guacamole. It was a grand Mexican-Jewish-American feast.

There were Californian wines, Cabernet Sauvignon, Pinot Noirs and Mexican beers, and lots of Coca-Cola, Tang and Fresca for the kids. The kids were set up in the backyard at our own table; again, left to our own devices. Food fights, fart jokes, burps, brief skirmishes and lots of laughter. Through the screen door I could hear the adults laughing and carrying on inside.

My father, bellowing from inside the house, called for my brother and me to come in to get some pie and cake to bring to the kid's table. We went inside, and from a table where some of the entrées had been there were now desserts. We helped ourselves.

I felt an odd feeling come over me, a sadness, and when this happened to me, I just wanted to be near my mother. I went over and sat on her lap. "My little GG," she said and brushed back the hair on my forehead and gave me a kiss. Meanwhile my father and cousins John and Chris were having a heated conversation.

"We had no reason to be there in the first place," my father was saying. Vietnam again.

"Oh yes, we did. The same reason you volunteered to go to Korea: to stop communism from taking over the world, to stop the dominoes."

My father was taking a sip of wine and almost choked on it. "I didn't volunteer, I was drafted. Korea was almost as big a disaster as Vietnam."

"But you didn't mind having your college education, or this house paid for by the G.I. Bill."

My father raised his glass. "I'll drink to that."

Uncle Dan spoke, "Korea was terrible, it is true. So many died; as many American soldiers died in Korea in three years to the ten years in Vietnam."

Chris raised his glass. "You served honorably, Uncle Dan, and you did too, Uncle Clint, whether you were drafted or not. And whether you agree with the war in Vietnam, you must respect that your country chose to be there."

My father put down his glass and got serious. "No, no I don't. It is just as patriotic to stand up and say that your country is making a mistake and is acting menacing to the rest of the world. I respect all the kids who protested the war more than I respect Richard Nixon. But don't get me wrong Chris, I respect you and your brother's service. One hundred percent."

Chris said, "Thank you Uncle Clint. Don't forget it was Kennedy, and it was Johnson who got us in the war."

"True enough," Dad said. "But it was Nixon who stayed and escalated knowing it was unwinnable and who bombed Cambodia without the approval from Congress and kept it a secret from the American people. Watergate is one thing, but he should have been impeached over what he did to Cambodia."

"Cambodia was hosting the Vietcong!"

"All right, all right," Uncle Dan shouted, practically crying, "That's enough!"

"Don't be upset, Uncle Dan. We are just having a lively discussion," Chris said.

"That's right, Danny," my father said chuckling.

Aunt Ozell said, "This dessert is delicious. What is it called, Maria?"

Maria looked up, surprised that she was being addressed. "It is called Tres Leches."

"Well, it is absolutely divine."

"Thank you. Would you like some more?"

"Oh. No thank you."

"Because I made plenty. It was Darrell's favorite."

Everyone got quiet at the mention of Darrell's name. People ate the dessert and took sips of their drinks. Suddenly Maria slammed down her fork on her plate. The plate cracked. "How can you talk about the war? How can you? The war is over! Your brother is dead. He died and for what? Your tone is disrespectful Robinson. Very disrespectful. You should be ashamed. But you are right. Darrell died, was killed brutally. For what? For nothing. For absolutely nothing!" She stood up and left the room. Uncle Dan went after her. I looked at my father, his face was flushed.

CHAPTER 67

It was a Tuesday night. It was raining torrentially. My father was not home for dinner. His Tuesday Kiwanis meeting. But Uncle Dan was there. Mom made what she liked to call her Mexican stir-fry, using the wok Dad had recently purchased to make what he called authentic Chinese food. Mom created her own recipe, most definitely unauthentic. She stir-fried serrano peppers, green onions, sweet red pepper, pork that she had marinated in pineapple juice, chili powder, garlic powder, oregano, cumin, salt, and pepper. And of course, cilantro, lots of cilantro.

My dad made fun of her Mexican stir-fry, but it was quite delicious. With warm corn tortillas, avocado, and black beans. Though Mom was not a "gourmand" like my father, she made good food, and never once did we have tuna casserole or bologna sandwiches on Wonder Bread as was the staple at all my friends' homes whenever I was invited for dinner. Which was not very often.

Uncle Dan was in a pleasant mood. He said he was looking forward to Christmas. He hadn't been drinking and was hoping that Maria would take him back for the holidays. But Mom told me that was not going to happen. Maria was probably never going to take him back, even though she still loved him. His handyman business was going well though, and Uncle Herman said he could help him find an apartment, but Mom wanted him to wait until after the holidays. In the meantime, he would continue to stay with us.

It was one of the Southern California nights that people wrote songs about, balmy and a steady pouring of rain. Before dinner, Kenny and I had been on the front lawn getting soaked, shirts off, in bathing trunks. The water felt warm slapping against my face. Kenny was being nice to me. And I was grateful for that. He sometimes liked to act the big brother and boss me around, but sometimes he also liked to act the affectionate big brother, putting his arm around me, asking if I needed help with homework or just staying with me outside longer than he wanted to play.

Before we started to eat, Uncle Dan said a prayer. This was something we did when Dad wasn't home for dinner. His prayer wasn't too long, unlike Papa Joe's lengthy prayers in Arizona for the big family gatherings. We sat with our hands clasped and heads bowed. "Dear Lord, thank you for this food. Bless the hands that prepared it. Bless it to our use and us to your service and make us mindful of the needs of others. Amen."

I finished my dinner and asked, "Can we watch TV?" Everyone looked surprised, pleasantly surprised, because even though I had started talking, I still barely spoke and hardly ever uttered any kind of request.

"Why, GG, you doth speak," Uncle Dan said laughing.

Mom reached out and touched my hand, smiled, and asked, "Did you finish your homework?"

After watching a couple shows, reruns of the Brady Bunch and the Partridge Family, my brother and I put on our pajamas, brushed teeth, and got ready for bed. Our room was in complete disarray. Toys, clothes, our baseball gloves, balls, and bats, building blocks, soccer balls, football, just everything scattered on the floor. Uncle Dan had built a big chest for us, so it didn't really take much to just clean up by throwing everything in there. We started the cleanup when Mom came into the room, put her hands to her face and said sternly, "Oh my goodness. I want this room picked up before you go to school tomorrow. Do you hear me?" My brother and I said we would. I put down my baseball bat and laid down in bed.

She pulled out the chair from our desk and sat down between our beds. We all said in unison, "Now I lay down to sleep, I pray the Lord my soul to keep, if I should die before I wake, I pray the Lord my soul to take. God bless…" And my brother and I took turns blessing all our family and friends. Even though my mom generally agreed with my father about organized religion, she still thought it was important to acknowledge a greater power, and this was the prayer that she was taught to say each night by her mother before she died of tuberculosis. She kissed us both, rather perfunctorily, on the forehead and left the room. We lay there for a while, in the darkness.

"Kenny?"

"Yeah?"

"Do you think the Angels will be any better next year?"

"I wouldn't bet on it."

"Why are they so bad all the time?"

"They have good pitching, Frank Tanana, Nolan Ryan, Ed Figueroa, but their fielding is terrible, and their hitting is even worse."

"Oh. Do you think that they will ever be any good?"

"Maybe. They just need to sign a few good heavy hitters, maybe trade some of their pitching for someone like Reggie Jackson."

I heard a noise. Sounded like maybe the front door. I figured it was Dad. I looked at the illuminated Mickey Mouse clock; it said 9:11. I never knew my father to get home that early on a Tuesday- Kiwanis night. Then I heard our dog Clive barking and then there was a muffled yelp. Feet shuffling, someone walking through the hallway to the TV room. It was not my father's walk. The door to the TV room opened, and I could hear the faint sound of the television. Uncle Dan would be sleeping in there on these rainy nights. Maybe it was Uncle Dan. But I thought he was in there already. Then I heard a bang, not loud, but powerful. I got up and went across the hall to see.

I went through the hallway and opened the door to the TV room. I saw Uncle Dan laying on the couch, blood dripping from his chest. I heard his strained breathing, like my brother when he had one of his asthma attacks. I turned to see the mangled, scarred head of Mr. Pacheco.

Mom rushed into the room, Mr. Pacheco threw his arm around her neck and told me to get back into my room. Mom screamed and pulled at this arm. He tightened it on her, and he told her to shut up or he would kill her. He was holding a gun in his other hand. He wore black gloves on both hands.

We entered my room, my brother charged at Mr. Pacheco, clawing at him. Mr. Pacheco threw Mom to the ground and slugged my brother in the face. He reeled back, landing at the foot of his bed, and passed out.

He told me to lie down on my brother's bed. He grabbed Mom and threw her on my bed.

"All right, family. It is time that you die. But first I am going to rape your mom. You see, that's what I must do whether I want to or not. Why? Because that is what the Suburban Killer would do. I'm not saying that I am the Suburban Killer, but if I were, that is what I would do. No, I'm not the Suburban Killer, but I have a theory that the Suburban Killer is a cop. Just a theory. Cops know how to get away with murder. That's why they have never caught the Suburban Killer. He knows how to get away with murder. I guess you know why I know that, because I know, that's all. GG—that's what your family calls you, I have heard them affectionately call you GG.

That's cute. I know Manny told you what he thought he saw, what he thought he saw. He thought he saw me killing his mom, me shooting his mom. It doesn't matter what he saw. All that matters is that it was his fingerprints on the gun. I think that he didn't even know for certain what the truth was. But. Yeah. I killed her. And killed Hector; it was so easy. Drove my former colleague's car and ran over the stupid kid. Drove it back to my former colleague's house and parked it. That cop, my former colleague, was a drunk and a junkie and everyone knew it. Homicide hit and run, what an animal. So, Manny thought he saw something, but it's not like anyone would believe a kid. Not when his prints were on the gun. Manny. Such a sad kid. How'd he get like that? His mom made him soft—with books and music, singing to him like she was some kind of angel. Like he was some kind of angel. He didn't learn how to be a boy. How to play football or baseball or learn how to swim. Manny didn't know how to swim; what was he doing in the swimming pool? I didn't put him there. But there he was, and it was so easy. I just put my hand on his head and then his shoulder and I held him down. You see, and I know you don't believe me, but Manny was my son, and I loved him. But I have another son, and another on the way, and it was for them that I had to kill Manny. And it is for them that I must kill you, all of you. That is, after I rape your mother. And I need for you to see that. Because, you see, you think that you are so smart, that you can outsmart what you consider evil, but that is not what this is, the intention is not bad or evil, it is about keeping order, but I know there is something in me—I recognize that, I can admit to that, to something evil in me. It has been there since I can remember." He stopped talking. Sweat was pouring from his forehead and salvia from the corners of his mouth. He looked around like he was hoping to find some place to sit down. He shook his head as if breaking the spell of his diatribe.

"I know I said I was going to kill you, all of you, but maybe I won't. Maybe I will." His breathing was heavy. Snot was leaking from his nose all down his face. A kind of yellow green snot. The kind of snot you have when you have the flu. He wiped it with his hand and threw it to the floor.

"Either way, you just sit still, or I will shoot you. I will shoot you. I can't rape her with my cock. My fucking cock was damaged by the exploding lawnmower. Was that you, GG? That was pretty sophisticated. You see, you're a little killer too. We all have that in us. All of us. I am going to have to use this gun. This hard, cold steel gun." Mom sat on my bed, her back against the wall. He came to her. Touched her thigh with the gun. Rested it there as he leaned in close to her face. Her face contorted, and she spat in his eye. He reeled back as if her spit was poison.

He screamed and I leapt at him. He threw me to the ground. Uncle Dan appeared from behind him, raised his hand, which was holding his army knife, and stabbed Mr. Pacheco in the back. Mr. Pacheco spun around, grabbed Uncle Dan by the shoulder, and threw him to the ground then got on top of him. He took the knife from Uncle Dan's hand and cut Uncle Dan's throat. I grabbed my baseball bat from the floor and slammed it hard against Mr. Pacheco's head. And I slammed it again and again. Until Mr. Pacheco collapsed completely. I lifted it once more to slam down on his prone and bloody head. I felt someone take hold of the bat. It was my mother. "That's enough, GG."

CHAPTER 68

I had wrapped my pillowcase around Uncle Dan's throat to stop the bleeding while Mom went to call for help. I crawled over to Kenny who lay prostrate on the floor by his bed. I rolled him over. "Kenny. Kenny. Are you alright?" He looked peaceful. As if all his anxieties, which I believed caused his rashes and asthma, had dissipated. I leaned over and kissed his forehead. He moved his head slightly, opened his eyes, the color- amber, and at that moment it was like I had never noticed them before, how striking they were. I had never looked down at my brother, looked down at him and into his eyes before and we stayed like that for a solid minute. He smiled and seemed like he was about to talk but he closed his eyes.

The cops and paramedics showed up and tookUncle Dan, my brother, and Mr. Pacheco who was remarkably still alive. I wondered if Uncle Dan was going to die, and if somehow Mr. Pacheco would get away with all of this. He had gotten away with everything already.

At the hospital, Uncle Dan was taken to the ICU, and my brother to another room. He had regained consciousness, but they still wanted to do some tests. Mom and I stood by his bed, and then my father showed up. His eyes were red. He was clutching himself. Arms Crossed. Mom hugged him, and his body untensed. My mother's hugs could do that. There was something magical about her touch. How could my father have a girlfriend when he had my mother's love?

We left Kenny at the hospital, but the doctor said we

could get him in the morning. And we drove in my father's Volvo. Jazz music was softly playing on the car radio. "I can't believe it. I can't believe that I almost lost you. That I almost lost my family. And GG, you were so brave, with your baseball bat." And I thought about that. I thought about how I had said to myself, after slamming Kenny's head to the floor, that I would never do violence again. But then I did. But I had to. You know. I just had to.

In bed, Mom held me firmly for a long while. And then she let loose her arms after she thought that I was asleep. My father was also sitting at the foot of my bed. They got up. I could feel their eyes looking down at me. They left the room.

I thought about Man, Manuel, Manny, and how I really liked him. I liked the kid in him. The kid who loved books and who wrote poetry and who knew about so many different things. A kid who was beautiful, really beautiful, unlike anything or anyone I had ever seen before. And how I could still see his face in my memory, as clear as anything. But I knew, in time, that would fade. And I remembered Uncle Dan quoting Saint Augustine, in remembering past joy we can hope for its return in the future, just as the remembrance of past sorrow instills in us the fear of impending disaster.

And as I was beginning to fall asleep, I thought I heard a clicking sound. I got out of bed; the clicking sound was coming from my brother's bed. I walked over and leaned down, moved the pillow that had fallen, and there was the yellow Panasonic tape recorder. The tape had come to the end of its side and was making that clicking sound. I turned it off and rewound it some. Pressed play, and there was Mr. Pacheco's voice: "Manny was my son, and I loved him, but I have another on the way, and it is for them that I had to kill…"

J.C. Hopkins is an American author, poet, painter, screenwriter and songwriter. He is the author of the novels *The Perfect Fourth, I Was a Teenage Communist, An Extraordinary Turn of Events* and multiple books of poetry. He is the screenwriter for the feature film *Poets Are The Destroyers,* winner in the best feature film category for the QueerX Film Festival and in the best comedy category for the New York Women's Film Festival. He has been twice nominated by the Grammys, for his song Dreams Come True, written for Norah Jones and Willie Nelson, and for his production of a children's album for actor John Lithgow. He also leads a jazz big band, the world renowned JC Hopkins Biggish Band.

www.ingramcontent.com/pod-product-compliance
Lightning Source LLC
Chambersburg PA
CBHW032243310726
48973CB00008B/2274